Good Vibrations

MARG MCALISTER

BLUE GEM PUBLISHING

ALSO BY MARG McALISTER

SERIES 1
Good to Go
Georgie Be Good
Good Riddance
Up to No Good
In Good Hands
Too Good to be True
As Good as It Gets
Good Golly Miss Molly
Good Vibrations
A Rocking Good Christmas

SERIES 2
Good Intentions
A Good Result
No Good Reason
Good Fortune

CHAPTER 1

Beach Babes

Georgie sipped the "Beach Baby Special" that Layla had concocted and sighed in appreciation. She wasn't sure what was in the pale mint-green beverage, but it was icy cold, fizzy, and delicious. Lying back in her reclining camp chair, wriggling her toes in the sun, she concluded that a laid-back week at Pismo Beach in California was just what the doctor ordered.

The weather was unseasonably warm—perfect for a beach rally in the fall—and right now, the sun was warming her skin while a light breeze played with the hem of her brand new, super-comfy draped pants from the Georgie B. Goode BoHo collection. The outfit was delicate and white and filmy and made her feel that she should be running in slow motion along the beach with white organza billowing out behind her, with her arms outstretched to greet a lover, who would, of course, be Scott…

"What are you smiling about?" demanded Tammy's voice, and Georgie heard a rustle as her friend and maybe-one-day-sister-in-law settled into the camp chair beside her.

"You just ruined a perfectly good fantasy," she said without opening her eyes. "I was the heroine in a romance movie. You know that running-to-meet-a-lover scene. The one that usually comes at the end."

"Oh, *that* scene. Well, don't let me disturb you."

"Too late. You already have. It was this fabulous outfit that Mags designed that did it. I had this urge to walk along the beach with the wind in my hair, but I couldn't be bothered getting up."

"Mags is a genius. It's gorgeous. Now open your eyes and see what *I'm* wearing."

"Let me guess." Beach party theme, thought Georgie. Tammy liked to pick songs from movies and dress to suit… "Maybe Annette Funicello…Beach Party…that white mesh two-piece swimsuit?"

"No, she's brunette."

"Blonde. Um. Beach party, beach party—Gidget Goes Hawaiian?"

"Close. Not Sally Field."

"Oh, I've got it. The *original* Gidget—Sandra Dee!" Georgie turned her head and opened an eye.

Tammy leaned back with her feet up, grinning,

wearing a red swimsuit with a white band across the top and three tiny red buttons. She drew a checkmark in the air and smiled. "Yep. But not the movie, the Coppertone ad." She wriggled and heaved a long, blissful sigh. "I can't believe this weather. I can actually bask in the sun in a swimsuit."

"It's going to be a perfect week," Georgie agreed dreamily. "A whole week to chat and shop and swim… but I don't think I'll risk the surf. I'll drown. The pool it will have to be."

"Pool later. I've been busy helping organize the entertainment; I need to rest." Tammy sampled a frosted drink in a glass identical to the one Georgie held. "Wow. What did she put in this? I can taste mint. There's soda. It has a Midori taste, but she said it's non-alcoholic…I don't know!"

"She wants us to guess." Georgie yawned. "I have a feeling it might take, say, three or four of these to identify the ingredients…what do you think?"

"Absolutely." Tammy went back to her entertainment plans. "We've got the absolute *best* 60s band. Two great vocalists; male and female. They're doing covers of the Beach Boys, Frankie Avalon, The Surfers, Dusty Springfield, The Supremes, Beatles… mostly beach party-type hits to fit the theme, but some other old faves. The dance party on the final night will have—"

"Let me guess," Georgie interrupted. "The

Mashed Potato. The Hully Gully. Um, the Twist, of course. Oh, and the Swim."

"Plus the Watusi and the Hitchhike. I'm impressed. Have you been browsing YouTube again?"

"No," Georgie said. "I've been watching *you* browse YouTube. You live for this stuff."

"I do," Tammy agreed happily. "So does Layla." She reached across to give Georgie a lazy poke. "And so do *you*. Admit it. You've been on the road for over a year now, visiting vintage rallies and reading fortunes. You're hooked."

"Not denying it." Georgie tipped the glass up to finish the last of her drink. "I might need another of these. Can we convince Layla to leave decorating her cake and join us with a nice iced pitcher of this stuff?"

"She said to tell you she'll be half an hour or so. Two people want to talk to her about the new hybrid vintage trailer from the RV Empire."

Georgie groaned. "She's not supposed to be working this week. We're all relaxing." She waved a hand at the palm fronds waving gently against the bright blue sky. "Look. Sun. Sea. Sky. All those good vibes. We have to go kidnap her."

Tammy lifted a languid hand to squint at a red and white 60s watch. "We'll give her half an hour exactly, then go and drag her away." She stopped and turned her head toward where they could hear a guitar tuning up. "Listen. The band. They're having a jam session outside their Kombi. Now it's even more perfect."

They listened for a few moments until a female voice started in on the Supremes' *Surfer Boy* and grinned at each other.

"Perfect," they both said together.

When Layla still wasn't anywhere to be seen after forty minutes had passed, Georgie finally sat up. "That's it. I'm going to get her. Don't let anyone else sit in my chair. I'm reserving it for about the next three hours."

"Done." Tammy sat up too and reached for the suntan lotion. "Unless it's Scott. He'll sweet-talk me into it. Or Jerry, who'll just take it anyway."

"Scott will give it up to me in a blink," Georgie said, "and if it's Jerry, all you have to do is fix him with That Look, and he'll do whatever you say. So I'm cool." She slipped on her sandals and picked up the empty glasses. "I shall return—with Layla and a pitcher of that divine beverage."

She made her way slowly back to her gypsy trailer, which was hooked up next to Layla's, pausing at one trailer after another to say 'hi' or to exclaim over the summer beach party themes. Evie Trent's gorgeous little white trailer painted with pink flamingos and palm trees held her up for a good five minutes alone, so it was fifteen minutes before she reached Layla's trailer.

She knocked on the door and poked her head in, grinning at the two women who were still poring over brochures. "Hi. Made a decision yet?"

"Hi, Georgie." Anita gave a mock frown. "Your father will have to stop coming out with these amazing trailers. They look vintage, but oh, the inclusions!"

"I know. He designed the variation on the Vardo caravan for me," Georgie said, gesturing to her trailer next door. "He should have been an engineer. Anyway…" she held up the two empty glasses and raised her eyebrows at Layla. "Are you joining us? Tammy and I need more of this magic potion, and *you* need to drink in that ocean view." She winked at Layla's two clients. "Sorry to drag her away."

"We've got enough here to keep us salivating all night," Anita said, gathering up the brochures and price list. "Can we steal a few more moments of your time at the end of the rally, Layla?" She looked a little guilty. "Sorry, I know this is not meant to be work for you."

"Not a problem," Layla assured her cheerfully. "I never get tired of talking retro. Honestly."

Georgie waited until the two women left, their eyes shining as they chattered about features of their prospective new trailers, and shook a finger sternly. "No more, Layla. From here on, it's all about relaxation." In the background, she heard the sounds of the Beach boys' *Fun Fun Fun* wafting their way. "Hear that? Perfect timing! It's all about fun!"

"Yes, Mom," Layla said, pretending to look chagrined. She took the glasses and rinsed them and then extracted a bottle of some green mixture from the fridge. "I'll just add soda and ice to this… can you get me some soda from the outdoor fridge?"

"Yep." Georgie got it and watched while she made up the pitcher of drink. "Are you going to tell us what's in it yet?"

"Not a chance. Chef's secret." Layla winked and slapped at Georgie's hand as she went to peek under a pink and apricot tea towel. "Stop that. No looking."

"It's the mystery cake, isn't it? Just a tiny peek?"

"No." Firmly, Layla barred the way. "It's a surprise." She sighed as the band launched into another Beach Boys number. "Listen to that. I feel as though I've stepped into a 60s beach party. Let's go!"

"*Good Vibrations!* There you go! I was saying to Tammy just a short time ago that this whole week had good vibes." She laughed, following Layla out of the door. "I must be psychic."

"Is that what it is?" Layla's voice suddenly cut off, and she turned to face Georgie as she had her foot on the step. "Don't look now," she said in a low voice, "but someone is waiting outside your trailer. And she's crying."

Georgie stopped dead and sneaked a glance out of the corner of her eye. Just a few yards away, facing away from them and dabbing at her eyes with a wadded-up Kleenex, stood a slim woman in denim knee-length shorts and a white cotton short-sleeved shirt left open over a burnt orange camisole. As they watched, she stuffed the Kleenex in the pocket of her shorts and stared at the closed door of Georgie's trailer.

"Looks like she's here to see you," Layla murmured. "Only trailer here that looks like it might have a gypsy fortune teller in residence."

Georgie sighed. "Dammit."

She knew before the woman said a word that it was happening again.

This was the reason she was here, apart from the sun, surf, and blue sky. She was always drawn to people in need.

"Remember what you told me," Layla said. "You're not here to work."

"Like you," Georgie said, "I don't have a choice."

Abruptly, the woman turned and saw them. Her face crumpled again as she took a few steps in their direction.

"I'm sorry." She moved closer, choking back the tears and fanning a hand in front of her face. "I'm sorry. It's this song that did it. It's just so *sad*."

Good Vibrations? Sad? It was one of the most cheerful songs that Georgie knew.

"I'll leave you to it," Layla said, commandeering the pitcher and the glasses. "See you later."

Georgie walked to meet the woman and took her by the arm. "You'd better come in and tell me all about it."

CHAPTER 2
Where's Marylou?

Her client made a heroic effort to regain her composure as Georgie let them both into the sunny interior of her gypsy trailer. Patterns of color from the stained glass window spilled across the table and the soft velvet seating, and the rich shades of crimson and ruby and grape in the drapes and bedspread glowed. It looked warm and welcoming, and Georgie hoped it would settle the distraught woman a little.

"Oh," she said softly, knuckling the last of the moisture from her eyes and gazing around. "Oh, it's so lovely in here. Is this…is this your home?"

"My home on the road. My home most of the year, actually—and one of my favorite places in the world. Take a seat." She touched the woman's elbow to urge her towards the bench seat and sat down with her. "My name's Georgie."

"I know. I read about you online last night, in the local news bulletin. They wrote a piece about the vintage Beach Party rally, and they talked about you —they said you had helped save Jaxx Saxby and then your brother from those preppers, and I thought…" she trailed off and bit her lip. "You don't have any signs out or anything, but I asked where to find you. You're probably not even doing any readings."

Despite her words, she looked at Georgie with hope in her eyes.

"I'm not hanging out my shingle if that's what you mean." Georgie met the woman's eyes. "But that doesn't mean I won't help you. If people need me enough to ask around and find me, then I'm here for them."

The woman's eyes welled with tears again. "You'll help? Oh, thank you. Thank you so much." Belatedly, she remembered that she hadn't introduced herself. "Sorry, I'm so rude. I'm Rosemary. Rosemary Scully."

Georgie reached for the Kleenex box, always handy on the small corner shelf, and handed it to Rosemary.

"Thanks." She blotted her eyes and managed a smile. She was lovely, with sun-streaked chestnut hair swinging in a neat bob around her chin and warm, dark brown eyes. Her lips were wide and generous, and when she smiled, a dimple creased one cheek. Full bangs swept her neatly arched eyebrows.

Without asking, Georgie got up, went to her small

fridge, and poured Rosemary a glass of chilled water. While the other woman sipped from it, she lifted down her crystal ball, still covered with its black velvet cloth, and set it gently on the table.

Rosemary set the glass on the table and swallowed, seeming to summon up courage for what was coming. "That's it? That's your crystal ball?"

Georgie nodded but left it covered for the moment. "Let's just talk first. Can you tell me what's worrying you?"

"Yes. Yes, of course." She inhaled deeply, gathered her thoughts, and started to speak. "My partner is a man called Shelton Crest. We live on the east coast, in Lowell—in Massachusetts."

"Okay," Georgie said encouragingly.

Her voice trembling, Rosemary said, "It's Shelton's daughter. She's missing."

"Oh." Georgie felt her heart miss a beat. *Not a missing child.* "I'm sorry to hear that, Rosemary."

"Her name is Marylou." Rosemary picked up her bag from beside her and flipped open the catch. She extracted a photo and turned it around on the table in front of Georgie. "In this photo, she's turning five, but she's closer to six now."

They both stared at the little girl in the photo, who was clapping her hands together in glee after blowing out candles on a birthday cake. The wisps of smoke were still curling in the air. She was a cutie, dressed up in a white party dress with a big hot pink sash around the waist. Her light blonde hair was caught up in bunches above her ears with two white scrunchies, and her brown eyes sparkled.

Rosemary reached over and gently touched the image of the child's face, her eyes inexpressibly sad. "It's breaking Shelton's heart."

"Of course it would be." Georgie stared at the picture of Marylou. "Can you tell me what happened?"

"Shelton's wife is…well. We think she perhaps has a mental condition. We can't say for sure; it's never been diagnosed or anything. But she's…" Rosemary shook her head. "She *twists* things. From what Shelton said, Paige puts on this reasonable front, and she sounds responsible and caring when she's talking to teachers, even Shelton's family. But she isn't like that at all. After she left, Shelton found she owed money everywhere, and she'd cashed in bonds." She seemed to shake herself. "But that's nothing compared to taking Marylou."

"So the child is with her mother?" Georgie frowned. At first, she'd thought maybe the child had been abducted or stolen away by predators, but this sounded like a family issue.

"We don't know. See, Paige used to take off for days at a time—sometimes weeks. She'd send a text message to Shelton to go pick Marylou up from pre-school or kindergarten, and then she'd come back when she was ready. Once, when Shelton was on a business trip, Paige left Marylou with a friend. He found the house empty when he came home, and then he got a phone call from the friend to come to pick her up." Rosemary hesitated. "It was a *male* friend. Shelton said he seemed very pleasant, and he doesn't think anything untoward happened, but still… we *think* she's with her mother, but we don't know."

"Rosemary." Georgie sat back. "I have to tell you; I don't feel comfortable with this. If you're worried about Marylou, shouldn't you involve the police? Or social services?"

"We tried," Rosemary assured her. "We've even hired a private detective, but there's no trace. If she's working, she's not paying taxes. It's as though she's disappeared off the face of the earth. The last time Shelton saw her was when—" Abruptly, her eyes filled with tears again, and she grabbed at the box of Kleenex. "We last saw Marylou was when Paige was driving off with her in the car, going to a fun park. A water park. And Paige had the radio up loud, and it was *Good Vibrations* playing, and Marylou was bouncing in her seat singing along…"

Now Georgie could understand her reaction when she heard the song. "Oh. So when you heard it just now…"

"I couldn't believe it. But then, maybe it was a sign. Maybe the stars are aligned, and we'll be able to find her again." Rosemary scrubbed at her eyes and shoved the crumpled Kleenex in her pocket to join the other one.

Georgie drummed her fingers on the table, thinking. She still wasn't sure about this, but if they'd tried police and social services and a private detective… what was left? How could she refuse?

Finally, she said, "You say you live in Massachusetts?"

"Yes."

"So why are you here? Why come to California to look for her?"

"Oh. Of course." Rosemary dug into her bag again and pulled out a tablet, turned it on, and quickly located a site. "Here. Take a look."

Georgie took it from her and immediately saw Marylou's face beaming out at her from a Facebook page. It was the same photo as the one Rosemary had shown her, but there were other photos as well. Marylou in a warm winter sleepsuit with Elsa and Anna from Frozen on it; Marylou careering down a slide at a water park with her father's arms wrapped around her; Marylou swinging on a tire suspended from a tree branch in a garden.

The caption was "MISSING - HAVE YOU SEEN THIS CHILD?"

"Shelton set it up a few months ago," Rosemary said. "The private detective suggested social media. He said it's one of the fastest ways to get results. We asked people to share it on their own Facebook pages, and now we've had three different messages from people who have seen a little girl like her around here… Pismo Beach and the Five Cities area." Rosemary's eyes shone with hope. "There were also a few leads from other parts of the country that came to nothing, but this time, who knows? So I flew out here and booked a hotel, and Shelton is wrapping up his business trip as soon as he can to get here."

"I see." Georgie nodded slowly. "And then you saw the local news item about me?"

"Yes. And I thought, why not? I mean, you might be able to tell us more about where to find her." Rosemary leaned closer, her heart in her eyes. "*Please*, Georgie. We just need to know that she's being cared for—and to give her the choice of coming home to her dad. We're not planning to snatch her back or anything…but we will have to call in the authorities; we can't just let her disappear again if we find her."

Georgie looked back at the screen in front of her; at little Marylou, her face alight with joy and her father, a slightly built, dark-haired man, laughing behind her.

She'd heard about parents who just ran off, taking a child or children with them, leaving a heartbroken spouse behind, not knowing what had become of them. Some left the country, and those were the most tragic cases—almost impossible to get back.

"No matter what you've heard, Rosemary, I can't

work magic," she told her gently. "I might see nothing at all—or I might find that what I get is all in riddles, something that won't make sense to either of us. I'm sorry, but there are no guarantees."

"I understand that," she said quickly. "But if you could just try…I know Shelton won't care what your fees are; he just wants his little girl back safely."

"I don't charge anything," Georgie said. She nodded at the fat pink pig up on a shelf. "I just take donations for the Red Cross. Whatever you want to give."

"We'll make a *huge* donation," Rosemary promised. She sat up tensely and patted her chest a few times as though to calm herself down as Georgie unveiled the crystal ball. "Oh my goodness. I'm so nervous. But excited too."

Georgie handed the tablet back to Rosemary and looked at the crystal ball. A few tendrils of white mist had already appeared in the center of the crystal. They slowly began to thicken and swirl around more quickly.

"Well," Georgie murmured. "I don't know what we've got here, but we do have something."

CHAPTER 3

An Unwelcome Visitor

Georgie focused on the shifting mist in the crystal ball and let her thoughts drift, concentrating on being open. The first thing she sensed was the generous and caring nature of the woman who sat opposite her. Rosemary's desire to find little Marylou was almost like a physical thing. Her warmth reached out, seeking to find and nurture, to make things better.

If they could find the child, Marylou was going to have a wonderful stepmother.

The mist slowly parted to reveal two faces. Clearly, they were mother and daughter. Although the images were slightly out of focus and shadowed, Marylou looked just as pretty as she had in the photos. She was looking up at her mother, Paige, and seemed to be asking a question. This time her light fair hair was loose, in one shining fall to her shoulders. She wore a bright blue Alice band.

Paige's hair was slightly darker than her daughter's, more the color of pale straw, and worn short. It was easy to see what Marylou would look like when she was older: there were the same deep-fringed brown eyes, the same straight brows, and determined chin. Even though it was like looking at a blurred photo, and her face was turned toward her daughter, Georgie would recognize her again if she saw her.

The crystal ball's perspective abruptly changed: instead of looking at two faces, Georgie could see both figures in full. Paige looked away from Marylou, as though seeing someone approach, and instantly stepped in front of her daughter. All Georgie could see was a swirl of Marylou's dress. Paige's face flashed into Georgie's mind: this time with eyes narrowed and calculating, her jaw jutting.

A third figure appeared, too shadowy to see any identifying features. A man…tall, bulky. He moved toward the other two and reached out a hand. Paige shook her head.

Marylou's face again, a quick flash, this time worried.

Then, nothing. Just mist.

Georgie's breathing slowed, and she closed her eyes, keeping what she had seen in her mind, searching for meaning.

They were nearby somewhere; she could sense it.

Maybe not living right here at Pismo Beach, but somewhere in the county. The people who thought they had seen Marylou were not mistaken.

Paige. She pictured the girl's mother, first looking at her child and then with that calculating look, pushing Marylou behind her. Hiding her.

Marylou, looking up, asking something, and then worried—just as the unknown male had approached.

What had Paige's actions meant, pushing the child behind her? She could be concealing the child from her father or shielding her from the unknown male. Or both.

One thing was clear: there was danger for Marylou here in San Luis Obispo County. Whether it was from a neglectful mother or the bulky stranger, or a combination of both, Georgie could not be sure.

She opened her eyes and looked first at the crystal ball, which was now clear, and then at Rosemary, sitting across from her holding her breath. Her anxiety was palpable as she arched a brow in query.

"I think you're right," Georgie said. "They're around here somewhere."

Rosemary exhaled, a long slow sigh of relief. "I can't believe it. Shelton has finally found her." She gave a shaky smile, and again the tears brimmed in her eyes. "Oh God, here I go again. I'm such a waterworks today." She pulled another Kleenex from the box and blotted her eyes. "I'm just so happy."

"Rosemary, I've got no idea where they are,"

Georgie said. "There could be over two hundred thousand people living in the county. More than that, I think."

"But we know where these people saw them. At a play center, at a mall. That's a starting point, right?" Rosemary was determined to be optimistic. "We can get the PI back on the job. And if you go to the play center, you might pick up something there...?" She trailed off and then had another thought. "If we gave you something that belonged to Marylou, would that help? I brought her *Frozen* sleepsuit and her little stuffed dog, and some other clothes."

Georgie, taken aback, had no idea. Nobody had ever asked her to locate someone by giving her some of their belongings before. "I don't know whether it works that way, but I could go to the play center with you. That might help. I'll take the crystal ball with me."

"Tomorrow?" Rosemary asked hopefully. "It's Saturday; that would be a good day to look at a play center. Shelton can't get here for a few days yet, but we can get started, right?"

Georgie spared a regretful thought for the lazy days of sun and chatter that seemed to be rapidly disappearing and nodded. "All right."

"I'll leave the photo with you in case it helps." Rosemary ferreted in her bag again. "Here's another one of Paige and Marylou together."

"Send me a link to the Facebook page, too," said Georgie.

"Sure." Rosemary put a visiting card on the table. "Here's my card; it has my phone number on it…and on the back, I've written the name of the hotel and our room number."

"And here's mine." Georgie handed her a card in return. "I'll phone you later to talk about times for tomorrow. Just let me think about all of this first."

Rosemary snapped her bag shut, looking considerably more cheerful. "I can't wait to tell Shelton. He doesn't know I'm here. I just thought I'd…" she trailed off and shrugged, covering with a smile.

"Check me out and see if I seemed legitimate?" Georgie asked, arching a quizzical eyebrow.

"Well, you never know." Rosemary flushed a little. "I didn't want to get his hopes up if nothing came of it. And I don't think he's really into this sort of thing."

"He wouldn't be the first," Georgie assured her, thinking of the many skeptics she encountered. "Let's just see what happens tomorrow, shall we?"

"Thank you. You have no idea." Impulsively, Rosemary stood up, leaned over, and hugged her. "If we can find Marylou and Paige, then Shelton can get divorced, and we can get married. He'll have his daughter back, *and* we can be a proper family. I'm so excited."

"You're welcome." Georgie squeezed her shoulder, touched. This was what made it so worthwhile; when she could make a real difference in people's lives.

She saw Rosemary out and waved goodbye, seeing her walk away with a new spring in her step.

Little Marylou: bright, vivacious…and missing a father. And possibly, she admitted with a cold feeling in her gut, in danger from the unknown male.

She would do everything she could to make this right.

Now she'd go and join Tammy and Layla and break the news: the Crystal Ball Investigation team had another case to solve.

Over where she had left Tammy minding her spot, there was now a small crowd. Tammy was still in her chair looking fabulous in her red Sandra Dee swimsuit, but she no longer looked relaxed. She was sitting upright, her gaze fixed on a voluptuous redhead next to her perched on Georgie's chair.

"Oh, no," Georgie muttered, her steps slowing. "You've got to be kidding." She closed her eyes briefly, but when she looked back, nothing had changed.

It was Jaxx Saxby. And now that her *Unsolved Mysteries with Jaxx Saxby* enjoyed such good ratings, she was sure to be more insufferable than ever.

Nobody had yet noticed her, so Georgie slipped

behind a shrub and watched through the lattice of green. The moment she went over there, Jaxx was bound to start hounding her again, urging her to change her mind about a gypsy fortune telling TV series.

She moaned. What was the woman *doing* here? Georgie and her team might have saved Jaxx from her stalker, but now she was becoming a stalker herself. Always on the phone wanting to consult about her unsolved mysteries, always in Jerry's ear about supposed problems with her new RV.

Agh.

Her eyes moved to the rest of the group. There was Seth, chief cameraman for the series, and Layla's long-distance boyfriend. He had a casual arm slung around Layla's shoulders, and she was grinning like a fiend. No doubt he'd kept this as a surprise for her—last Georgie had heard, Layla wasn't expecting to see Seth again until Christmas.

Also in the group was Dominic, the second cameraman, and Ella, Jaxx's long-suffering PA and hairdresser. Georgie was surprised that she was still around after the way Jaxx had treated her.

There was no sign of Lilli Chin Lee, the producer. And neither Seth nor Dominic had a camera with them, so at least they weren't shooting the vintage rally.

She hoped.

"Dammit, dammit, dammit," she muttered again,

clenching her fists in frustration. The week by the sea she'd looked forward to so much had been hijacked - first by Rosemary and now by Jaxx.

Rosemary, she didn't mind so much; she really liked her.

Jaxx was a completely different story.

Well, standing there fuming wasn't going to help. She'd just have to face the music.

CHAPTER 4

Georgie Holds Firm

Georgie was almost upon them before Jaxx spotted her and jumped up with a squeal, flicking back her abundant red tresses and lurching forward on super-high heels to fall into Georgie's arms. "Georgie!"

She was wearing a short, tight black skirt made of something shiny and clingy and a lime-green tank top that dipped low over her full breasts. Over that was a fine mesh cardigan in black with some sort of glitter thread worked through it, tied at the waist. Her strappy sandals, Georgie noted as she hastily stepped back to avoid being spiked, had four-inch lime-green heels.

As always, Jaxx barely escaped looking like a street-corner girl touting for business.

Georgie submitted to the hug and smiled back through gritted teeth. "Jaxx. How are you?"

"I'm *so* glad to see you again!" Jaxx smacked a kiss on both of Georgie's cheeks and beamed at her. "My favorite psychic!"

"Fortune teller," Georgie corrected, looking around to check that none of the rally attendees were within hearing range. Faint hope. It seemed that the word was spreading, and already people were popping out of trailers to see the famous Jaxx Saxby in person.

She wanted to kick Jaxx. It was a waste of time denying that she was Jaxx's 'secret psychic' consultant if Jaxx trumpeted it to the world.

Like Georgie needed any more media coverage.

Layla caught her eye and winked, making a sympathetic face. She was no keener on Jaxx than Georgie, but Jaxx being here meant that Seth was, too. She could put up with Jaxx to see more of Seth.

"So," Georgie said, sliding around Jaxx and taking possession of her camp chair before Jaxx could hijack it again. "What are you doing here in Pismo Beach?"

"I was hoping you'd ask." Jaxx looked around for a chair and took Layla's, on the other side of Tammy, tugging ineffectually at her tiny skirt as she sat down. She leaned across Tammy to continue the conversation, ignoring her. "We've got a haunted house here, and a missing will, and heirs that are at each other's throats—perfect for ratings! I need you to come with me to do a reading at the house. So exciting!"

"No," Georgie said. "No publicity, Jaxx. That's the condition of any help I offer."

She pouted. "*Georgie.* C'mon. If we shoot you in silhouette? That'd work. Be even better." Her face brightened. "We could do it like that car show. *Top Gear.* Have you seen it? They have an ex-racing driver or something who races around a track with celebrity guests and always wears a full helmet. So, like, nobody knows who he is. The mystery psychic." She nodded enthusiastically. "I like it."

"She's talking about The Stig," Seth supplied, his lips twitching. He tilted his head to one side, looking at Jaxx. "You want Georgie to wear a helmet?"

"Don't be obtuse, Seth," she said haughtily. "We'll do the silhouette thing. Or she can speak from behind a curtain."

Georgie looked around for something to bang her head on. "Jaxx, NO."

"We'll talk about it later," Jaxx said. "I'm sure we can work out *something.*"

"We're busy all week." Georgie waved a hand around at the vintage trailers, stretching out in rows with their beach-themed outdoor settings. "Tammy's been organizing this Beach Party rally for months. There's a heap to do."

Jaxx waved aside such unimportant considerations. "You can borrow Ella. She can help Tammy while you help me."

Tammy bared her teeth. There was no way it

could be mistaken for a smile. "I really need Georgie."

Jaxx sent her the barest glance of acknowledgment. If a look could be made of ice, this one would qualify. She considered Tammy to be her archrival for the affections of Jerry. B. Goode, heir to the vast Johnny B. Goode RV Empire. It mattered not a whit to Jaxx that Jerry had rejected her attentions on countless occasions. "Jaxx and Jerry" sounded just perfect to her, as she had confided to Layla.

And he was the only stunningly handsome man she knew who also had buckets of money. She hadn't shared that with him or his family, but Seth had overheard her talking to a friend and had passed it on to Layla, who naturally had told Tammy and Georgie.

"Can't happen, Jaxx," Georgie said, her voice louder than usual. "I've promised Tammy, and besides, I have some important things to take care of myself." For a second, the image of young Marylou's face flashed into her mind. Locating the little girl and her wayward mother was way more important than any flashy TV production Jaxx Saxby might come up with.

Jaxx looked as though she was about to argue, but then her eyes narrowed. She sat forward, a move that made her skirt ride up even further. "Things to take care of? Are you on another *case?*"

Inwardly cursing the media coverage that had made such a big deal of her using her crystal ball to solve the Jaxx Saxby stalker case, Georgie looked back coolly and shook her head. "I'm here for fun and relaxation this week, Jaxx." Which, she reflected, was true enough—she just hadn't counted on another desperate client. "But I do have a few personal things to sort out."

Jaxx tapped one long nail—lime green with silver sparkles on it—on her teeth and gave a skeptical nod. "If you say so." She continued to stare at Georgie, plainly suspicious.

The woman had an absolute *radar* for intrigue, Georgie thought in dismay. She'd have to make sure that Jaxx didn't get a whiff of what she was up to, or she could ruin everything.

Jaxx and a camera crew following her around while she tried to locate a missing child?

If ever there was anything to guarantee failure, that would be it. Paige and her daughter would be off like scalded cats, and that would be the end of any hope of Shelton being reunited with his little girl.

Fortunately, just then, Jerry turned up, which served nicely to deflect Jaxx's attention. Her face brightened, and she leaped to her feet again, teetering on her sandals. "Oh, look! Here comes Jerry. I haven't seen him for weeks, and he's been so *good* about fixing anything that goes wrong." She shot a triumphant look at Tammy—with a scathing glance at the retro swimsuit, which would undoubt-edly cover entirely too much flesh for Jaxx's liking—

and turned to Jerry with both arms outstretched. "Jerry!"

Layla smothered a giggle while Tammy looked on inscrutably.

Jerry shook off his initial deer-caught-in-the-headlights expression and plastered on a full-wattage Jerry. B. Goode salesman-type smile. After all, Jaxx had spent over a million on her new motorhome—and had sent millions more in orders his way from her wealthy friends.

He couldn't afford to get on the wrong side of Jaxx Saxby. Not many people could.

"It's good to see you, Jaxx." He submitted to a Jaxx's enthusiastic greeting, manfully submitting as she planted a juicy kiss right on his lips. "How's the RV doing?"

"Wonderful. No problems since you fixed that problem with the leveler thingies," she told him, holding on to both of his arms. "I'm having a teensy celebration tonight. My birthday. You must come!"

"Uh…" Jerry shot a desperate glance around for help but was met with nothing but poorly disguised amusement from Layla and Seth and a yawn from Dominic. He freed himself from Jaxx and peered around her to Tammy. "Um, I, um…do we have something on tonight, Tammy?"

"*I* do," she informed him. "I'm the chief organizer. But *you're* free, sweetie-pie." She tipped down her red-framed cat-eye sunglasses and smiled at Jaxx, who had turned around to look at her. "He'd be delighted to attend, Jaxx. We can't have you celebrating your birthday alone. What can he bring?"

Jaxx released her prey and put her hands on her hips, a movement that made her breasts jiggle in the tight green top. "I'm not celebrating it *alone*, Tandy. I've got some *brilliant* friends coming." She put her nose in the air. "And Jerry doesn't need to *bring* anything. It's *catered*, of course."

Georgie didn't know anyone else who spoke in italics as much as Jaxx. With every word emphasized, she managed somehow to pout her full red lips suggestively.

Porn star looks, she thought. Jaxx was in the wrong line of work.

"It's Tammy, actually, not Tandy." Tammy pushed her sunglasses back on her nose and got to her feet with one easy movement, which was easy since she was barefoot instead of balancing on insanely high heels. In her 60s Sandra Dee Coppertone ad swimsuit, she managed to look effortlessly classy and elegant compared to Jaxx in her glitter and neon camisole. Smiling sweetly at Jerry, she leaned forward and brushed a thumb over his lips as if to wipe away Jaxx and then patted him on the cheek. "You run along and have a lovely time, darling. And don't forget to make time this afternoon to pop out and pick out something nice for Jaxx. There are some lovely jewelry stores in Pismo Beach." She glanced at Jaxx's glittery mesh cardigan. "Something sparkly, I would think."

Jerry looked appalled. He finally found his voice. "Didn't I promise to help you out, Tams? I don't think…"

"Nonsense. In fact, you know what?" Tammy beamed at him enthusiastically. "Why don't you spend a bit of time with Jaxx while she's here? She's right; you haven't seen her for *weeks*." She picked up her towel and tossed it over her shoulder, collected her sunblock cream, and theatrically consulted her retro watch. "Look at the time. I've got to get going." She smiled sweetly at Jaxx. "Happy birthday, Jaxx, and have a *lovely* evening." She leaned closer and whispered something to her, and Georgie saw Jaxx shoot her a suspicious look from under lowered brows.

Tammy walked away, the towel over her shoulder swaying with each movement of her trim hips, stopping to exchange greetings with those who were standing around pretending they weren't there to catch a glimpse of the famous Jaxx Saxby.

Jaxx looked triumphant.

Jerry looked sick.

Layla abandoned Seth and sauntered over to Georgie. Picking up her Beach Baby Special in its frosted glass, she bent down close to Georgie's ear, mirth dancing in her eyes. "Did you hear what Tammy said to Jaxx?"

"I couldn't quite catch it. You were right next to them. Was it a warning?"

"Not unless you know Tams as we do," said Layla. She took a sip and checked to make sure that Jaxx wasn't listening and said in a low voice, "She told Jaxx that Jerry was shyer than he looked, so he'd need a bit of encouragement."

Georgie hid a smile and regarded her brother, who was listening with half an ear to Jaxx's plans for her birthday party. He wore his usual easy smile as he nodded and twinkled at her – but Georgie caught the glance he shot after Tammy when Jaxx turned to ask Ella a question about the catering. For an instant, Jerry looked like a dog that had been kicked.

It was kind of nice to see him in that state, after the hell he'd given her when she was a teenager.

"Perfect," she said. "Jaxx will eat him alive."

"Yep," agreed Layla with satisfaction. "Tammy wins again."

Suddenly, Georgie felt a whole lot better.

CHAPTER 5

Seth Springs a Surprise

Preparing for the early evening beach party, Georgie dressed in an ankle-length tiered cotton skirt in rich shades of burnt orange, red and yellow. The waist and a deep V at the front were trimmed with complex embroidery inset with glowing stones in amber. It didn't exactly say 'sixties', but the BoHo look suited her gypsy trailer and felt like *her*. She teamed it with a simple off-the-shoulder white top with long sleeves in deference to the cooler night air.

Before she met up with the vintage crowd and got caught up in chatter and laughter and stories about road trips, she needed to phone Rosemary.

Her new client picked up immediately. "Hi, Georgie." There was a lightness to her voice that hadn't been there the day before—and a new sense of resolve.

"Hi, Rosemary. I just thought I'd better call before

I disappear for the evening. You know how it goes when the social whirl starts."

"I phoned Shelton. He's thrilled. Well…" she hesitated and amended it to "I mean, he's encouraged, but he still doesn't like to get his hopes up *too* much."

"And he's especially not convinced that a gypsy fortune-teller can find out anything?" Georgie guessed, keeping her tone light.

"I have to be honest. He's placing more faith in the PMs on Facebook, and he's going to contact the PI again, but he's kind of impressed by what you've done. He looked you up online while we were talking, so he knows you're not one of those flaky ones."

Georgie felt her lips quirk in amusement. "I like to think I'm not."

"He said I should go ahead and check out the play center, but not to do anything until he can get here. He *especially* doesn't want us to do anything that might frighten them away."

"Very wise. I feel the same way," Georgie said feelingly, thinking of Jaxx Saxby. "How about if I pick you up at your hotel at, say, one thirty tomorrow? Saturday afternoon would seem like a good time to catch kids there."

"Terrific. I'll be waiting at the entry, so you can just cruise in and pick me up." Rosemary's voice had been getting progressively more excited as she spoke. "We're going to find her. I just know it."

"I really hope so. See you tomorrow, Rosemary."

Georgie ended the call, crossed her fingers, and held them up in the direction of the crystal ball. "Here's hoping."

She picked up a platter of nibbles—Scott was providing the wine—opened the door, and shrieked to find a shadowy figure standing there.

"It's only me," Seth said quickly, taking a step back. "I was just about to knock. I didn't mean to frighten you."

Georgie pressed a hand to her chest. "You just took about ten years off my life." She thrust the platter at him. "Here, take this for me while I lock up." She glanced back at him. "Where's Layla?"

"Helping Tammy set things up. I took the opportunity to come and see you while she's busy."

Her curiosity piqued, Georgie joined him and held her hands out for the platter. "That sounds interesting."

"I'll carry it." He cleared his throat. "I came to enlist your help. I…" he coughed and then said in a rush, "I'm going to ask Layla to marry me."

Georgie stopped dead. She turned to face him, a smile of delight already splitting her face. "What? Really?"

He nodded, grinning back, pleased with her reaction. "Yep. Think she'll say yes?"

"Of course she will. She's nuts about you. Why else would she be heading off to join you at every possible opportunity?" Georgie rose on tiptoe and planted a kiss on his cheek, causing Seth almost to drop the platter. "I'm so thrilled. *She'll* be so thrilled." She had a million questions about how this was all going to work, but in the end, it meant she would be losing a member of her road team. *That* sucked. Layla would naturally want to be where Seth was.

"Anyway…since she's so crazy about this whole vintage scene, and all her friends are here, I thought it would be the perfect setting. So when Jaxx had to come out here to set up this mystery thing with the missing will and all for her show, I thought, this is it."

"Brilliant idea," Georgie agreed enthusiastically. "Wow, this is going to be so much fun. What a finale! How long are you all going to be here?"

"Several weeks—we'll still be here after the rally." Seth's steps slowed, and he nodded down toward where Jaxx had her huge RV parked, party lights blinking outside. "Can we just go down here for a minute while we talk, not over where Tammy and Layla are?"

"Sure." Georgie detoured with him. "You've got your own motorhome now, haven't you?"

"Just a small one, but well-designed. Nothing like Jaxx's palace." His voice held amusement. "Mine's the silver-gray and black one, three down from hers."

"Noisy evening for you," Georgie said, hearing the music and laughter drifting their way. "You're not going to the party?"

"You're kidding. We're just the crew. I'd rather be over with you guys anyway."

"Let's go back to your place and talk, then."

They made their way to Seth's motorhome. Inside, it was sleek and modern but still homey and welcoming. Georgie smiled at the cushion on the charcoal seats. Embroidered in bright, fun colors, it featured a vintage trailer. "Layla's handiwork?"

He picked it up and moved it aside with a smile. "She says she's got to have *something* of the retro world around her when she stays here."

Georgie sat opposite him and beamed. "I almost turned and ran when I saw Jaxx here, but I'm always happy to see *you*. And especially happy now. Tell me what your ideas are?"

Seth ran a hand through his tousled sandy hair and shrugged, looking a bit lost. "I want it to be perfect for Layla. You and Tammy, you know her so well, I thought you'd be able to suggest how to make it special. How can I set it up to surprise her?"

Georgie thought for a moment. "Do you two have a special song? Movie? Something that has meaning?"

"Not really. If you pick a song that she likes, and it's associated with her engagement night, then *that* will be special, won't it?"

"I like the way you think. I'll get some ideas from Tammy—oh, have you said anything to Tammy yet?"

"Layla's always around—and I know she's got a

million jobs to do; she said she might not be able to spend much time with me until the rally's over if I'm trailing around after Jaxx, and she's setting things up here. That's why I thought you'd be better; you can plan stuff without her getting suspicious."

"That's true…" Georgie nodded thoughtfully. Things were working out, actually: while the others thought she was busy helping Rosemary track down her partner's daughter, she could be organizing Layla's engagement party.

Layla's *engagement* party. The thought sent a delicious thrill through her. She beamed at Seth again.

"What?" he said, smiling in response.

"It's just all so *romantic.*" She ran through possible music in her mind. "I can line up something with the band. Maybe *Everybody Loves a Lover.* They'll enjoy joining in." Suddenly she sat bolt upright. "That's it. *Everybody Loves a Lover*! That can be your song. And Tammy can sing it just like Doris Day; you should hear her! Perfect!" She slapped the table.

"Okay." Seth nodded, looking pleased if somewhat panicky. "Okay, great."

"The last night of the rally, I think. Everyone's really in party mode then, and all the hard work will be over. Layla and Tammy will be able to relax." And, she thought, with any luck, she would have located little Marylou by then. "I'll organize a cake. And engagement presents. This will be the best beach party-slash-engagement party ever!" Then she had another thought. "Do you have a ring?"

"Not yet, but I know her ring size," he said. "I traced around a couple of her rings one day when she was out."

Georgie sat back and grinned. "You've been planning this for a while."

"It kind of came into my mind when she last came to visit," he admitted, unable to keep a goofy grin off his face. "I was thinking maybe Christmas, but then this came up, so…" he shrugged.

"We have to go shopping for the ring," Georgie decided. "I think I know what she likes, so if you get something she likes *and* you like, that'll do it. I'll quiz her a bit…very subtly, of course." She nodded, satisfied. "Okay. I'd better get along to the party, or they'll be going to fetch me. Are you coming?"

"They're expecting me too," he said. "I just had this little detour to make."

"Then let's go. I can't *wait* to tell Tammy."

"Do you think she'll be able to keep it a secret?"

"Absolutely."

Seth followed her outside, and they walked past Jaxx's RV, hearing her infectious laughter as they went by. She was, Georgie had to admit, charismatic. It was only those who had to work with her who were driven crazy.

She glanced up and saw Jerry on the other side of the window, nodding and smiling at someone as though there was nowhere else he would rather be than right there at Jaxx's party. Somehow, she doubted that…but he'd do what he had to.

"As long as he does the right thing by Tammy too," she muttered, heading on up to where the real party was happening.

Seth had seen the direction of her glance. "Jerry?"

"Jerry."

"I don't think you need worry," he said surprisingly. "He's told me a few things."

Intrigued, Georgie glanced at him. "He has? What?"

"My lips are sealed. Secret Men's Business." He mimed, zipping his lips and grinning at her.

"Huh." It was turning out to be a busy week, Georgie thought.

All she had to do was juggle a vintage rally, find a missing child and organize a surprise engagement party.

Piece of cake.

CHAPTER 6

Jaxx the Stalker

What a night. What a morning. The rally had barely begun, and Georgie's head was already spinning. The night before had been a cheerful riot of singing along to 60s jukebox hits, trying to master the Watusi and the Swim (with lots of mistakes and hysterical laughter), eating, and drinking.

Scott could do the Watusi. Who would have thought? And the Hucklebuck. She'd never heard of the Hucklebuck, but he said his Mom was a Hucklebuck master, and he'd grown up knowing how to do it.

The things you found out about people.

Then she had sworn him to secrecy and confided Seth's plans for the surprise marriage proposal. "Be ready," she warned. "He might need some support on the night."

"A marriage proposal," Scott had said with a glint in his eye. "Hmm. We could make that two."

"We could not," Georgie told him firmly. "This is all about Layla."

He just smiled and tilted his bottle of Bud at her. "I am going to marry you one day."

"So you told me," she said, "soon after we met."

"You haven't said no."

Georgie just smiled at him and kissed him on the forehead. "No, I haven't said no." And she wouldn't say no, because of *course*, she was going to marry him, but the time didn't feel right. She'd know when it was right.

"Just be prepared," she told him, "to run interference whenever I need it. If I tell you it's a Layla emergency, invent a reason to distract her."

"Yes, *sir*."

Tammy's reaction had been everything she'd hoped for. Georgie had chosen her moment. Tammy had just come off the stage after belting out Little Eva's *The Locomotion* with the beach band and had sunk into a chair, kicking off her shoes. "Water. I need water. Then wine."

Georgie provided her with a glass of iced water, then a glass of champagne from a bottle she'd begged from one of the rally attendees.

"Champagne?" Tammy frowned at it and tilted the glass to watch the bubbles rise. "I'm not a champagne type. I'm the wine type. *You're* a wine type. Why are we drinking champagne?"

After checking that Layla was nowhere near, Georgie leaned over and whispered, "It's for a toast. A *secret* toast. Ready?"

Tammy's eyes widened. "Scott has proposed."

"Nope. Well, yes, but he does that regularly." Then Georgie thought again. "No, he doesn't. He just says, "I'm going to marry you one day" at various intervals. I must point out to him that that is *not* a proposal. Anyway, I keep saying *not yet*."

"Jerry also asks regularly," Tammy said. "All kinds of ways. He always gets a no. Does that mean we're just contrary?"

They grinned at each other.

"So," Tammy said, eyeing the bubbles rising in her champagne flute again, "what *are* we celebrating?"

"Don't react when I tell you," Georgie warned.

"I am a blank slate. Now, *what?*"

Georgie let it play out for a long moment, enjoying Tammy's impatience, and then leaned closer. "Seth," she said, "is going to ask Layla to marry him."

Tammy's mouth parted in a perfect "O". For a moment, she was speechless. Then she shrieked, "YAHOO!" before clinking her glass against Georgie's and tossing back a mouthful of champagne that had her coughing and spluttering a second later.

George rolled her eyes, grinning, and drank to the moment. "Nice non-reaction, Tams."

The next moment Layla was heading their way.

"What's got you two going?" she called out when she was still several paces away, and then, her face puzzled, "are you drinking *champagne?*"

Georgie went blank. Uh-oh.

Tammy had regained her composure. She grinned at Layla. "A glass for you, too!"

"Well, of course. I'm the only one of us who *drinks* champagne. Not you two." She eyed them suspiciously. "What's up?"

"It's Jerry," Georgie said quickly. "I, um, just told Tams that when I walked past Jaxx's RV, I spotted Jerry in there helping to celebrate her birthday. He looked like he was lining up for the hangman's noose. So Tammy decided that was worth toasting in champagne."

Tammy looked at her. Georgie had no trouble interpreting that look. It said: *You just lied to Layla.*

Georgie never lied. Well, not to her friends. And now she had lied to both of them because Jerry had looked quite happy and composed.

She wasn't so sure that she liked being the repository of secrets after all.

"Oh, sure," Layla said, "I'll drink to *that.* Got another glass?"

Tammy tipped her champagne flute in the direction of the side table containing the champagne bucket, the bottle, and a tray of glasses. "Right there. Help yourself."

While Layla stepped across to pour herself a good splash of champagne, Tammy leaned forward. "Tell me again," she suggested sweetly, "about how *miserable* Jerry looked…?"

Georgie tipped up the glass and drank some more.

"Georgie," Tammy said patiently.

Georgie sighed. "He looked just as sociable as he always does. Well, what was I supposed to say? It's all your fault she came over here. You *shrieked*. I had to say *something*."

"Being sociable, huh? That's what I thought." Tammy sounded quite cheerful. "I would have been disappointed if I'd called it wrong. Fits with my plan."

"You didn't tell me you had a plan."

"It's only a half-formed plan." Tammy saw Layla turn to come back with a brimming glass and mimed 'bring the bottle!'

Layla waved, pivoted, and grabbed the champagne bucket.

Tammy grinned at her and Georgie while Layla topped up their glasses.

"Another toast," Tammy said. "To all good men and true."

Layla happily echoed her words, blissfully ignorant that she was the actual subject of the celebration.

Now, the morning after, Georgie was battling a slight champagne headache while entering Rosemary's hotel address into the GPS and trying to get her mind focused again on a missing child and a bereft father—instead of engagement plans and the fact that she had agreed to meet Seth at 3.30 that afternoon to help choose a ring.

First things first.

A missing little girl.

She drew in a deep breath and turned out of the RV park.

Jaxx Saxby watched Georgie head off along the road and pursed her lips. If there was one thing she prided herself on, it was her nose for a story. Her new series proved it. *Unsolved Mysteries with Jaxx Saxby* had been twice as much of a hit as her also-popular series, *From Little Things*, which had brought her into contact with the Goode family ----------

And its 8th generation gypsy fortune-teller, Georgina Bridget Goode.

Georgie had proved to be her secret weapon when it came to solving three of those mysteries. And while it was kind of cool having people trying to guess who her 'secret psychic' was, it would have been even better if Georgie would just agree to appear in each segment.

That didn't seem like it was ever going to happen. Jaxx, snorting in annoyance at the thought of Georgie's stubbornness, thumped the steering wheel. Well, if Georgie wouldn't cooperate, then Jaxx had no option but to do a bit of detective work herself.

She might not have a crystal ball, but she could follow the person who did.

Come to think of it, that made her, Jaxx Saxby, a detective in her own right. Nobody could track down a story as she could. Giving herself a little pat on the back, she flipped down the sun visor to check her appearance in the mirror—telltale red hair hidden under a baseball cap, oversized sunglasses, casual tee-shirt—before nosing out of the RV park to set off after Georgie.

Georgie wasn't as smart as she thought she was. Jaxx Saxby knew a lie when she heard one.

Her secret psychic was covering up something, and Jaxx meant to find out what it was.

Rosemary was, as she had promised, ready and waiting outside her hotel. Dressed in jeans and a loose asymmetrical top, with a roomy handbag slung over her shoulder and a bulging plastic shopping bag in her hand, she waved and jumped into the car.

"I don't know how you plan to handle this," she said, "but I brought some photos of Marylou. I thought we could show them around, ask people. Is that all right?"

Georgie ran through it in her mind. Yes, they wanted to know whether people had seen a little girl like Marylou... but they didn't want to raise any flags.

"We need to be careful not to frighten her off. Let's just start by sitting there and watching for a while. See if I pick up anything; you never know."

Rosemary's head swung toward her. "What do you mean? Did you bring your crystal ball? To the *play center?*"

The astonishment in her voice made Georgie laugh. "Don't worry; I'm not going to set up in a corner and grab random people for a reading. I just like to have it with me."

"Wouldn't it be amazing if we *saw* her?" Rosemary wriggled in her seat. "I've watched Shelton's home videos over and over—the ones she left for him, that is. Do you know she took the laptop with her, with all their home movies? How cruel is that? He still has some on his desktop computer and one on his phone. I'm sure I could recognize Marylou instantly. I know her *voice.*"

"And if we *do* see her?" Georgie asked cautiously. "What then?"

"That's what I said to Shelton last night. What if I see her? I *can't* just let her go."

"You can't just take her, either," Georgie warned. "You'll get arrested."

"Can we follow them? If we see them?" Even as she said it, Rosemary raised both hands in a 'whoa' motion. "Sorry. I'm running ahead of myself. I've been over and over this. If I call the police, do I tell them that she's been kidnapped from the other side of the country? *Is* it kidnapping if she's Marylou's Mom? Shelton says I should play it cool; just get a photo of the license plate and photos of the two of them. He can give it all to the PI." She sank back in her seat, fanning herself. "He doesn't think I'll see them anyway. We couldn't be that lucky."

Georgie pulled up at a set of traffic lights and checked the GPS. The play center wasn't far away. She looked over at Rosemary. "Let's just wander around and look for a while when we get there. Get a sense of who goes there, what they do. Don't move too quickly. Let me do my thing, Rosemary."

Rosemary swallowed. "I will. I promise. I'm not going to ruin everything." Her voice trembled. "And I don't want to frighten Marylou. I might feel as though I know her, but she doesn't know me. To her, I'm just a stranger."

Again, Georgie felt the good-heartedness of the woman beside her. She reached out and squeezed her shoulder. "Hang in there. We'll find her. We will."

Rosemary nodded and sighed. She reached down and showed Georgie the plastic shopping bag. "I brought some of her clothes—and her doll, Elsa from *Frozen*. And there's a tee-shirt of Shelton's that he says she liked to wear to bed. You can take them with you, see if you get anything from them."

"I'll try, but as I said, I haven't done that kind of thing before." Georgie shot a look at the bag Rosemary held and thought of the little girl who had owned all those things, pushing aside a nagging, horrible feeling that danger was moving ever closer to Marylou.

From her mother—or from the shadowy male she had seen with them?

One thing at a time.

First, *find* them.

CHAPTER 7

No Mary Lou

The play center was enormous. It was divided into age-appropriate areas for babies, toddlers, and active kids of school age, with plenty of tables in each area where supervising adults could sit. There were slides, climbing frames, a miniature road for cars and trikes, and a soft play area spilling over with colored balls.

The place was buzzing with children's shouts and laughter.

Georgie looked around, wide-eyed. "Wow. I've never seen anything like this."

"Play centers are great. I've been to one like this back east, with my sister and her kids. We grab a coffee and catch up while they run and play." Rosemary turned in a slow circle, clearly hoping that she'd see a familiar little girl with light blonde hair.

A thought struck Georgie. "Does Marylou's mother know anything about you?"

"I don't think so. I didn't meet Shelton until six months or so after she left."

"That's good. If she's here, then she won't recognize you." Georgie looked around her, trying to think of what might appeal to a six-year-old girl. "Marylou liked the water-slide, didn't she? So she'd probably like the big slide over there in the corner." She pointed. "And maybe the video games. Don't all kids play those now? And we could try the Three Bears cottage."

"Okay. Oh, I'm so nervous."

They started with the two giant slides, side by side, watching children of all shapes and sizes whizzing down. Their cover story, should they need one, was that they were assessing a range of indoor play centers to find a good meeting place for a mothers' playgroup.

Rosemary didn't just look; she got involved, chatting to the mothers and making laughing comments to the kids.

"You're good with children," Georgie commented as they crossed to the Three Bears' Cottage. "You must spend a bit of time with your nephews and nieces."

"Just nieces," Rosemary said. "Five of them between my two sisters. Marylou will have plenty of kids to play with." She was starting to get quiet. "I don't think she's here. A couple of times, I thought…" she shook herself. "It was too much to hope for."

Georgie could feel the weight of her crystal ball in the bag over her shoulder. It rested against her hip, where she would be able to feel it if the temperature changed. It had done that when they were driving to Kentucky to find Jerry, months before, and had given them a lead.

So far, she'd felt nothing—no change in temperature, no tension in the air to signal that she was on to something.

"What do you think?" Rosemary asked when they took coffee back to an empty table right at the back of the room. "Should we start asking around? Show her picture?"

"And say what?" Georgie queried.

Rosemary sighed, knowing what she was getting at. "If we say we're looking for a missing child, and word gets back to Paige, she'll run. Can we maybe say we're looking for a friend and her little girl?"

"Why would we be showing everyone a picture instead of just looking around? It might look suspicious."

"Yes, right." Rosemary sipped her coffee, her brow furrowed. "What about the staff? Tell them we're supposed to meet a friend at a play center but we can't remember which center it was, and ask if she's been in today? If she's a regular, they might recognize her." She snapped her fingers. "I've got a couple of photos on my phone that Shelton sent to me. I'll use one of those. Would that look more convincing than showing around a printed photo?"

"Probably. It's worth a try."

In the reception area, there was a constant flow of parents and children arriving or departing and two people at the desk to take money or sell small items from the attached gift store. They waited until the girl at the desk was free, and Rosemary moved forward, flipping open her phone as she did so.

"Hi," she said with a bright smile. "I'm supposed to meet my friend at a play center this morning. I have a feeling I might be at the wrong place. Can you tell me if they've been in?"

The photo on her phone showed Marylou with her mother, taken at the same birthday party as the photo Georgie had seen of Marylou blowing out candles. Paige was watching her daughter opening a present.

The girl took the phone and turned it around to look more closely. "Oh, yeah, they come in sometimes. Not today, though. What time were you supposed to meet up?"

"I thought it was two o'clock." Rosemary looked up at the huge clock on the wall. "It's half an hour past that already. Either I've got the time wrong, or she's not coming."

"Or the *day* wrong," Georgie put in. "Are you sure she didn't say Sunday?"

"Surely not." Following the cue, Rosemary took the phone back from the girl and asked, "Do they usually come in on Saturday? Or Sunday?"

The girl shook her head. "I'm not sure. It's always so busy here."

"Thanks anyway." Somewhat discouraged, Rosemary put her phone back in her bag.

"Maybe she hangs out with somebody here who could tell you," Georgie suggested. She waved a hand around, looking at the girl. "Is there anyone here you've seen with her?"

The girl barely glanced at the crowded play center, concerned more about the people queuing up behind them. "Not that I recognize."

"Thanks anyway." Georgie gave her a nod and took Rosemary by the elbow. "Come on. Let's go check out some of the other centers, just in case."

As they left the building, Georgie could see that Rosemary was disappointed, although she tried to be philosophical about it. "I was expecting too much. Of course, she wasn't going to be there."

Georgie unlocked the car. "Good idea, to use the photo on your phone. That's more convincing than be carrying around a photo in your handbag."

"Thanks. Are we going to the other play centers?"

"We can if you like," Georgie said, "but I thought we might try the mall. The other Facebook lead?"

Rosemary slid a glance at Georgie's bag, resting at

Rosemary's feet with her handbag. "You don't want to try the crystal ball?"

"Not yet. We already know that Marylou comes to this play center, so we're getting closer. You can always get Shelton's PI to stake it out," Georgie pointed out. "Let's go to the mall. You never know your luck."

She entered the second destination into the GPS, and they headed off.

Jaxx stayed in the reception area for a moment, where she'd stood with her back to them listening while she pretended to read brochures about hosting birthday parties at the play center. Allowing them time to move away from the door, she hurried outside. She couldn't afford to give them too much of a lead.

Georgie's family truck with its maroon canopy was just pulling out of its car space. Jaxx was relieved to see a queue of several cars at the exit, waiting for a break in the traffic. That should hold them up for a few moments.

She slid into her car and started it up, thinking about what she had overheard in the reception area. It was clear that Georgie and the unknown woman were looking for someone. At a play center, that was sure to be someone with a child—unless they were looking for the child itself. A boy? A girl? Rosemary hadn't said; she'd just asked about the 'they' in the photo.

This had the distinct smell of another Jaxx Saxby unsolved mystery: she just *knew* it.

Joining the queue, she was only one car back from Georgie. Wherever they were off to now, she'd be right behind them.

At the mall, they wandered around for half an hour, visiting the children's department in various stores and taking a good look in cafes.

"This is hopeless," Rosemary said finally. "It's like looking for a needle in a haystack. They could be walking down one aisle while we're looking in the next."

"I have to agree." Georgie was only half paying attention. There was a spot between her shoulder blades that itched. No, she couldn't describe it as an itch. It was as though something had touched her there.

She shivered and hunched her shoulders together briefly.

There it was again.

Was someone *following* them?

She stopped abruptly and turned around.

A short distance behind them, she caught a glimpse of a woman ducking into a store.

"What is it?" Rosemary, realizing that Georgie wasn't still beside her, had turned and come back.

"I'm not sure. Did you notice anyone listening in while we were asking about Paige and Marylou?" Georgie kept her eyes fixed on the store entrance where she'd seen the woman disappear.

"No." Quick on the uptake, Rosemary scanned the Saturday afternoon crowds. "You think someone's following us?"

"Maybe. Let me just check something."

Georgie backtracked to the store and peered in through racks of men's t-shirts and casual pants. There was an older woman toward the back, comparing two different pairs of pants, and a bored-looking man going through a rack of suits. She shifted her gaze to the side wall, where there were rows of shirts on two levels of hanging rails. A woman in a baseball cap and loose t-shirt was standing with her back to the entrance, studying a pale lemon shirt she had partially drawn out.

A tendril of red hair had escaped from under her cap.

Georgie narrowed her eyes and swore under her breath.

It had better *not* be.

She slipped into the store and walked over to the woman, moving in right next to her.

Dammit!

"I wouldn't buy that one," she said conversationally, reaching out to rub the fabric of the shirt between thumb and forefinger. "Jerry's not that into yellow shirts. And it looks cheap."

Jaxx gave a reasonable facsimile of a start at Georgie's first words before looking at her with a wide smile. "Georgie! Imagine running into you here." She pushed the shirt back onto the rack. "Oh, I'm not buying it for *Jerry*."

"No?" Georgie pretended polite interest. "Who, then?"

"Oh, nobody in particular. I'm just buying and putting away for Christmas."

"Without knowing a size?"

"The large size fits most of the men I know," Jaxx said dismissively. A familiar look of calculation entered her eyes. "Anyway, since we've run into each other, want to grab a coffee?"

"Not really," Georgie said. "I'm a bit pushed for time." She looked at her watch for show and then realized that she did have to meet Seth in less than an hour to pick out a ring. This day was a complete bust so far. "I've got to get going."

"Anyway," Jaxx said, "what brings *you* out today?"

Georgie smiled. "Like you, early Christmas shopping."

Jaxx rolled her eyes, and then her gaze fixed on something over Georgie's shoulder. A slow smile grew on her face before she shot a smug look at Georgie. "Aren't you going to introduce me to your friend?"

Georgie turned around to see Rosemary standing there hesitantly, watching them.

"No," Georgie said. "See you around, Jaxx. And please don't follow me, this time."

Jaxx, ignoring her, pushed past to hold out a hand to Rosemary. "Hi. I'm Jaxx, a friend of Georgie's."

Rosemary's mouth dropped open. "Oh goodness. I know who you are. Of course I do. You—the stalker —Georgie…"

"Got time for coffee?" Jaxx asked, moving in with the instincts of a shark. "You have the look of someone with a story worth hearing."

CHAPTER 8

Totally Gorgeous

Outside the first jeweler they had agreed on, Georgie spotted Seth waiting for her, shifting nervously from one foot to the other. His expression cleared somewhat when he saw her truck drive past.

"Sorry I'm a bit late," Georgie said when she reached him. "Had to do a bit of damage control." She could hear the banked fury in her words, but she couldn't help it.

Jaxx Saxby was the biggest pain the rear end she had ever met. *Ever.*

"How can you work for her?" she burst out. "I mean, really, Seth, how *can* you?"

"So that's why you look ready to eat someone alive. Jaxx bugging you about doing that show again?"

"Worse," Georgie told him as he held the door open for her. "She's poking her nose into a new case. *Mine*, not hers. And she's such a pushy idiot that she could ruin everything." Inside the store, she stood with her hands on her hips. "Do you know she *followed* me today? Honestly, what's with her?"

Seth's expression of wry empathy changed to one of shared irritation. "She does that, I'm afraid. It's got her into trouble before this."

Georgie growled and then abruptly recalled the purpose of their outing. "Let's not talk about her. We're here to pick out a ring." The thought of helping to choose an engagement ring for Layla did lift her spirits somewhat. "Have you thought about what you like?"

"I've thought about what *Layla* likes. I'd use the ring-pull from a soda can if that's what she wanted."

"You can forget *that* idea." Georgie saw a sales clerk coming toward them. "Here we go! The first day of the rest of your life."

He stopped her with a gentle touch. "Working for Jaxx was a career move—but it's about to end. So that you know, I have no loyalty toward Jaxx if you need help."

"Thanks." Touched, Georgie reached up and kissed him on the cheek. "I might rope you in when I calm down enough to think of a strategy."

"Hi there." the sales clerk greeted them, smiling at the demonstration of their affection. She glanced at Georgie's bare finger and then at Seth. "How can I help you today?"

"A ring." Seth drew a meaningless circle in the air with his forefinger. "Uh, engagement ring, that is."

"Congratulations!" She beamed at them both and then raised an eyebrow at Georgie. "Do you know your ring size?"

"Oh, it's not for me. I'm just the help," Georgie assured her, laughing. "Seth?"

"Here." He pulled a crumpled piece of paper from his pocket and handed it over. "She had different sizes, but this is the one that she wears on the third finger – but on the other hand. Does that matter?" He extended his hand toward her. "It fits on my little finger if that helps."

"It could," she agreed brightly. "Now, do you have anything in mind?"

Seth swallowed. "She likes old-fashioned stuff."

Georgie took pity on him. "Layla," she told the woman, "likes vintage clothes, vintage jewelry. She attends a lot of retro events."

"And she sells vintage trailers," Seth supplied, trying to help.

The woman exchanged a quick look with Georgie and dropped one eyelid in the vestige of a wink. "We've got some back here that might interest you. Let me show you."

An hour and twenty minutes later, after being in and out of half a dozen jewelry stores only to go back to the first one to make the purchase, they were standing in the street next to Seth's hire car. He had a smile from ear to ear and hair more tousled than usual from having a hand run through it dozens of times in the decision-making process.

"It's right for her, isn't it? Really?"

"It's *perfect*. I knew it was the moment I saw it, but we had to compare." Georgie smiled at him, liking him enormously. Good-hearted, witty Seth would be just right for Layla. It was so satisfying seeing your friends find the right man. "I think you knew it too, didn't you?"

He nodded enthusiastically. "I did. It has that old-fashioned look that she likes, and lots of her rings are that pinky-gold."

"Rose gold. One of my favorites, too." Georgie held up her phone, which held a picture of the exquisite heart-shaped engagement ring with intricate butterfly shoulders. "Tammy will be bursting out of her skin to see it—and the matching wedding ring. Don't be surprised if she has me keep Layla busy so she can come and get a proper look at it."

"Thanks again." He hugged her and held up the small white bag closed with a gold ribbon. "Step one accomplished. Now all I have to do is get through the proposal." Seth looked a little sick. "She'd better not say 'no'."

"She won't. Don't worry; we'll be there to hold you up. So will Scott, if you need a male. I'll catch up with you tomorrow about the final plans for the evening."

She watched him drive away, her mind already drifting to Rosemary, Marylou, and the latest complication.

Jaxx Saxby.

Again.

Well, if nothing else, the Jaxx problem would be the perfect way to distract Layla.

As it happened, the RV park was quiet when she returned. All the preparations for the community meal and talent quest-slash-open mic were in hand, and a good many of the rally attendees—many of whom were still recovering from the night before—were resting up before the evening festivities.

Georgie made her way directly to Tammy's cheerful scarlet and white trailer, decorated for the occasion with red, white, and navy bunting. Four director's chairs grouped around a white table wore navy slipcovers, and on each one was a cushion—red, navy, or white—boasting an embroidered anchor. On the table, next to a hurricane lantern, there was a red vintage radio and some artfully displayed magazines featuring vintage trailers. Tammy being Tammy, she had found a faded copy of a popular 60s magazine and some old vinyl records with Hits from the Sixties sleeves.

Tammy always left things set up as though she was setting the stage for a photoshoot. No wonder she had transformed the Jerry B. Goode Vintage trailer section so that sales were at an all-time high.

She tapped on the door, and Tammy whipped it open instantly, motioning her inside. "At last! Tell me, tell me! I've been dying to hear. Did you get a photo?"

"Yes, but I told Seth you'd probably be over to look at the real thing."

"Layla's waiting for him in his motorhome, so I hope he doesn't walk in with Tiffany's bag or anything."

"More interesting than Tiffany's. Look." Georgie dug out her phone and showed her the ring.

"Oh." Tears sprang to Tammy's eyes. She swiped them away and then looked again. "It's gorgeous. Totally gorgeous. Did he choose it himself?"

"Yes. He knew what she'd like. He only needed me along to confirm that he was choosing the right thing." Georgie's lips quirked. "He told the sales clerk that she liked 'old-fashioned stuff' and 'things made of that pinky gold.'"

"I like a man that pays attention." Tammy took one last look. "Forward it to me, will you, so I can look at it whenever I like?"

"He's proposing tomorrow night," Georgie reminded her. "After that, you can grab Layla's hand and look your fill."

She sank onto one of Tammy's bright bench seats. "I need coffee. Otherwise, I'll never stay awake until tonight. I also need to update you on Rosemary." Warily, she sneaked a look at Tammy while her friend busied herself at the coffee machine. "*And* on Jaxx's latest antics."

Tammy's hand slowed for a second, and then she clicked the coffee capsule lid shut with a decisive *snick*. "Oh, yes?"

"Nothing to do with Jerry," Georgie said quickly. "But she's sniffed out that I'm on to something. And today, believe it or not, she followed me—first to Rosemary's hotel, and then to the play center, and finally to the mall, where we busted her." She wriggled back with a heartfelt sigh, kicked off her shoes, and leaned against the wall, her feet drawn up on the end of the seat. "I need a plan. We've got to keep her out of the way until Rosemary finds Marylou. You know what Jaxx is like: she generates publicity by *breathing*."

"She needs to be clapped in irons," Tammy said, jabbing at a button and watching the coffee streaming out.

"That's for sure. Maybe we can handcuff her to the stabilizer legs of her precious RV," Georgie said venomously. "The Jaxx Palace. Did you know that's what she's calling it?"

"I heard."

"Or we can lock her in. Drug her?" Georgie groaned and looked hopelessly at Tammy. "Now she's got me contemplating a life of crime. Next thing, I'll be on a show about the secret psychic that went feral."

Tammy streamed coffee into a second cup. She had a faraway look on her face. "So that's why Jaxx wasn't around this afternoon. I wondered why Jerry was hanging about being so attentive."

"How did he enjoy the birthday party?" Georgie asked, momentarily diverted.

"I think it was all right. He managed to evade Jaxx's advances—he was careful to let me know that —and two of the people who were present are flying to Elkhart so he can design an upmarket motorhome for them."

"Can't he ever *relax*?" Georgie watched Tammy at work pouring in the stretched milk, carefully manipulating the pour as a barista had taught her to get a leaf shape on the top. She marveled again at the strange pairing: Tammy the rockabilly princess, always gorgeous and charming in vintage clothes— albeit a mean hand with a gun—and Jerry, a born grifter with a broad streak of self-interest that had given her grief all through childhood.

Tammy, sweet and generous with a core of steel.

Jerry, manipulative and charming and a con man extraordinaire, with a soft heart for Tammy and nobody else.

Maybe they *did* suit.

Tammy, bringing the coffee to the table, lifted an eyebrow. "What are you pondering now? I can see the wheels turning."

"Just trying to figure out you and Jerry."

"*I'm* still trying to figure out Jerry and me," Tammy told her. "But you gave me another idea. You want Jaxx kept out of the way?" Her eyes gleamed. "I know just the way to do it."

CHAPTER 9

A Revelation

Tammy took her time going to Jerry's motorhome. On the way, she dallied to pass the time of day with Judy in her 61 Shasta compact trailer and exclaim over the accents of turquoise and red, and two sites further on to sample Laverne's special lemonade outside her gorgeous little pink-and-white trailer—yet another Shasta. Over much laughter and pretended reluctance, she finally agreed to swap Layla's Beach Baby Special recipe for Laverne's lemonade recipe, *provided* she didn't pass it on to anyone else… "or otherwise Layla will kill me!"

She walked on with a smile on her face, thinking how much she enjoyed her retro friends and the whole scene. Why everyone in the country didn't want to be part of it was beyond her comprehension.

Then she came to Jerry's black and gold motorhome and stood looking at it for several minutes. *This* was why everyone in the country didn't want to be part of the retro scene. Some people liked huge sumptuous leather lounges and fridges as big as the ones in their kitchen and two bedrooms and marble bathrooms and slide-outs.

That was Jerry. His taste was about as far away from tiny vintage trailers as you could get.

She tapped her lips thoughtfully. To be fair, she had to admit that there were times when she, too, liked to stretch out and relax in sinful comfort with an icemaker on tap and a giant TV screen.

But overall? She was content with her soft, comfy bed in her little vintage trailer. And even then, she was cheating, really, because it was a Johnny B. Goode vintage design that combined a good many modern comforts with the retro look she loved.

A movement caught her eye, and she realized that Jerry was watching her through the window. She pointed a finger at him, grinned, and climbed up the steps.

The door swung open, and he drew her in, wrapping his arms around her and kissing her.

Tammy had to steel herself not to melt. If Jerry B. Goode knew precisely the effect he had on her, it would give him way too much power. She allowed herself to get lost in the kiss for about three seconds and then drew back, putting one finger against his lips. "That'll do. I'm wearing all-day lipstick, but I'm not sure just how Jerry-proof it is."

"You can put on another coat," he said, urging her back again.

"Uh-uh." She planted a hand against his chest and gave a gentle push. He groaned and sat on the lounge, shaking his head. "You're killing me, Tams."

She sat on his knee and adjusted the collar of his polo shirt, which didn't need any attention at all, and patted his cheek. "How was the party? Apart from the guys who are flying to Elkhart to commission multi-zillion-dollar motorhomes? I didn't get a chance to talk much this morning."

He looked at her warily. "It was noisy. Pretentious. Full of social climbers."

"Yet you have another little dinner party tonight, I believe?" She smiled. "Just you and Jaxx this time?"

"What? Not that I know of." A slight hint of panic showed in his eyes.

"Oh, that's right, she hasn't asked you yet." Tammy inspected her fingernails. "I ran into her by the pool, only I don't think it was an accident, and she told me that she's arranging a tete-a-tete with you this evening."

"Well, perhaps she should have checked with *me* first," Jerry said, sounding nettled. "I was planning on being at the communal dinner. You *know* that, Tams. I was helping with the cookout."

"She has offered Seth's services to help with that —since, as she pointed out, he would be there with

Layla anyway. I said that was fine; that you'd love the chance of getting away from all those noisy, uncouth retro people."

"Tammy." His eyes went cold. "What in tarnation are you up to? Pushing me at Jaxx? *Why?*"

"It makes a change from trying to persuade you to stay away," she said coolly, pushing herself off his lap. "When are you going to start telling her that you're simply not available?"

"It's *business.* I keep telling you that. You know how much she's worth to the RV Empire."

"Jerry, she's playing you."

He heaved an irritated sigh. "When will you understand that it's nothing to do with Jaxx? The woman is a constant thorn in my side. And it doesn't help for you to be shoving her in my face all the time."

"Then tell her you're not available. She bought a motorhome, which as far as I know didn't come with you in the contract as her flunky."

"You're being unreasonable."

"In that case, enjoy your meal with her tonight." Tammy smoothed a hand over the hips of her high-waisted shorts and tucked in the matching striped shirt with a crisp collar, knowing this would draw his attention to her slim tanned legs and tiny waist.

A girl had to use what weapons she had, after all.

"Fine," he snapped. "*Fine.* I will. And you make

sure you enjoy yours. I think you'd rather be with your vintage friends than me anyway."

Ow. That stung. Tammy kept her expression calm. "Perhaps you could do me a favor, Jerry."

"Oh, now you want a favor? Blowing hot and cold here, Tammy."

"I'm serious." She stepped forward and put a hand on his shoulder, capturing his eyes. "You owe Georgie. You know you do."

He blinked. "Georgie? What's Georgie got to do with this?"

"She's got a new client, and Jaxx has been sniffing around. She followed Georgie today, and she's going to jeopardize everything. We need you to keep her away."

"Tonight?" He looked at her through narrowed eyes. "Is that what this is all about? You're making it all about me when you're really trying to help Georgie?" He shook his head and huffed out an annoyed breath. "Between you and my sister, honestly!"

"Just do it, Jerry, will you?" Tammy was becoming just as irritated, but she didn't want him to see that he was getting to her. "Do I have to beg?"

"No, Tams, you don't because begging's not in your nature. Sometimes you can be really cold, you know?"

She looked at him, shocked.

Cold? *Cold?* How could he even say that? He knew her better than that.

Then a swift flash of hurt in the back of his eyes, barely there before it was gone, gave her pause.

He really thought that?

Tammy hesitated and then reached down and took his face between her hands. "Please do this for me, Jerry," she said softly. "Please?"

Anger warred with indecision in his eyes. Then he gave one short, sharp nod. "Just tonight, then."

"Thank you." She leaned forward and kissed him again and then nipped his bottom lip between her teeth.

"Ow!" He pulled back. "What was that for?"

"A warning," she said. "I've seen Jaxx go into full seduction mode. If you let her get any closer than *this* —", holding her hands about six inches apart, "then you're *toast.*"

She left him staring at her and sashayed out of the monster RV and back to her retro crowd.

Yes, she loved being with them, she told herself.

But not more than she loved Jerry.

Damn his hide.

Jerry couldn't help himself. He went to the door to watch her walk away, her trim hips swinging and her blonde Sandra Dee hair bobbing.

His heart turned over.

She meant the world to him—the *world*. And Jerry B. Goode had never thought he'd say that about any woman.

He thought about Jaxx, with her voluptuous figure and her botoxed lips and her provocative clothes. She was more intelligent than people gave her credit for, and sometimes she amused him, but he hated how she manipulated people.

There was no honesty in Jaxx.

Tammy was pure gold.

What the hell was he thinking? He had enough money already never to have to work again… and all Tammy wanted was a little ten thousand dollar trailer and enough money to dress it up like a doll's house.

That, and a good man who wouldn't hurt her.

Suddenly, he saw himself through her eyes.

He had to fix this.

CHAPTER 10

Rosa Pops In

When Scott let himself into her trailer, Georgie barely heard the door open. She knew it was him without looking and half-raised a hand to beckon him in.

Rosa was driving her nuts again.

Scott clicked the door gently shut behind him and leaned against it, watching.

"It's Rosa," Georgie said, peering into the crystal ball with a frown. "The strangest thing. I felt her urging me to get out the crystal ball. I expected to see her face in it, but—nothing." She looked up. "I *felt* it, Scott."

He stayed where he was. "If she wants to tell you something, all she has to do is phone."

"Well, I know that," Georgie said in exasperation. "But Rosa's Rosa. She hates using the phone. Any *normal* person would do it the simple way, but not

Grandma Rosa. No, she just pushes suggestions at me that come flying out of nowhere, and then—as *usual* —she leaves me to figure out what she means. What *it* means." She nodded at the crystal ball and pushed it away.

Scott came to join her at the table. "Did you get the sense that it was urgent?"

"Yes." Georgie looked at her watch. "Right now, when I'm due to go help Tammy and Layla at supper? *Now?* Seth's over there flipping steaks and burgers, and Layla's making gallons of her Beach Baby Special, and they've lined up the talent quest, and I'm supposed to be the MC…"

Laughing, Scott captured her hand in his. "Nothing's going to fall apart if you're not there for fifteen minutes, half an hour. The talent quest isn't for another hour." He checked the time. "Hour and a quarter."

"But I don't know what Rosa *wants.* I've tried focusing on Rosemary and Marylou, but all I can think about is Jaxx getting in the way, although Tammy says she's put Jerry on the job to distract *her,* and…"

Her tirade was interrupted by the buzz of her phone.

"Maybe that's her. Maybe she's finally going to just *talk* to me." Georgie snatched up her phone. "No, it's Rosemary… hi, Rosemary."

"Georgie." Rosemary sounded nervous. "I'm

sorry if I'm a pest, but I had to phone. Look, I told Shelton about Jaxx Saxby, and he is anxious that she's going to barge in at the wrong time and frighten Paige away. Can you stop her? Jaxx, I mean, not Paige."

Georgie closed her eyes and drew in a deep breath. "I'll certainly try, Rosemary, but you've met Jaxx. She just barrels on through and does what she wants."

"Shelton says even if you can delay her for a day or two, just until he can get here, and maybe get his PI on the job..?" She trailed off and then said in a rush, "You know, I didn't like her all that much, Georgie. I know you do all that work on her show, and she's famous, but she's not like she seems on TV, is she? She doesn't listen, and she just—"

"I know. She just rolls right over the top of you." Georgie swiftly ran through a few options. "She won't do anything tonight, Paige, because we've got Jerry watching her. That's my brother. And tomorrow..." she made a sudden decision. "She's been bugging me for months to do an interview, do a segment for her show, so I'll agree to that on the condition that she leaves you alone."

"Would you do that? Oh, *Georgie*. Thank goodness. I was only trying to help, coming out here early, but I thought I might have ruined it all for Shelton. For Marylou." Rosemary's voice wobbled.

"I promise I'll keep her off your back, Rosemary."

"Thank you. And…one more thing…did you try to get anything from Marylou's clothes?" She waited for a beat while Georgie rolled her eyes at Scott and then said, "I know you said you don't really do that, so it's okay if you haven't. I just thought, you know, anything that might help…"

"I'll do it tonight. It might not be until late because things here are a bit busy, but I'll do it."

"Will you phone me if you get anything from them? Even if it's late?"

"Right away," Georgie promised.

"Thank you so much. Well, I'll go. I'm sorry to load this all on you, Georgie. You've been so good, and I know this is work for you."

"Not at all." Georgie felt another pang of sympathy for Rosemary and Shelton. They had been battling on by themselves for months, trying to get people to help, so it was the least she could do. "I'll be in touch soon."

She terminated the call and looked at Scott. "Jaxx freaking Saxby. I will honestly kill her."

Scott sat back and looked at her quizzically. "You're going to agree to an interview on camera?"

"Yes, on the condition that Seth does the filming. And then he's going to, unfortunately, find that the camera card or hard drive or whatever he uses is inexplicably corrupt. *That'll* fix her."

"Well." He gave her his slow smile, amusement

growing in his warm brown eyes. "You're becoming a devious woman, Georgie B. Goode."

"I know." She glanced back at the crystal ball and jumped out of her skin. Rosa's face was there, staring at her intensely. "Yikes. *Now* she's here."

Scott leaned forward curiously, watching.

Georgie drew the ball closer, opening her mind. *What?*

An image of Rosemary's face floated into her mind, but she didn't appear as an image in the crystal ball.

Something else did, though.

Elsa, the doll from *Frozen.*

Georgie spun around and looked over to where she had tossed the bag of clothes on the bed. "The clothes?" She looked back at Rosa's face. "The doll? What?"

There was a feeling of being thumped between the shoulder blades, and then Rosa's face disappeared.

Georgie gritted her teeth. "She might be in her nineties and my family, but I could strangle her sometimes."

"Strangling great-grandma, killing Jaxx, you're going to be busy," Scott said mildly. "I'd put both of them out of my mind and just focus on Marylou."

"Yes." Georgie wearily leaned her chin on her hand. "You're right, of course."

Scott went over to the bed, picked up the bag

from Rosemary, and stacked everything in it on the table next to the crystal ball.

They both looked at the sad pile of mementos. A Frozen doll and sleepsuit, the dress from Marylou's fifth birthday party, a small pair of pink sneakers with glitter laces, and a dark blue much-washed man-sized t-shirt with BEST DAD EVER on it.

"Go on," Scott said. "Everything else can wait."

CHAPTER 11

Jerry Stuns Them All

Georgie looked at the pile of things in front of her and reached for the Elsa doll. "A doll. Little girls hug their dolls a lot, don't they? We'll see if this gives me a clue about where she might be."

The doll was soft, with worn patches on the arms, and its dress had a tiny tear in the skirt. This, Georgie thought, was a toy that had been loved, not one that spent its time on the shelf.

Georgie caressed the dress's fabric with one hand and drew the crystal ball closer with the other. Her eyes went to the photo of Marylou that rested on the table and then back to the crystal ball.

Slowly, Marylou's face took shape in the soft mist that only a few minutes before had revealed Georgie's great-grandmother. Rather than smiling as she had been in her birthday photo, Marylou's little face looked serious, and there was a sadness in her eyes. "I bet she's missing her father," murmured Georgie. She stared at the little girl's face. "Where are you, Marylou? Help us to find you."

Marylou just kept looking at her steadily, still unsmiling. It was as though Marylou was waiting for her to work something out. Georgie ran through what she knew of Marylou. It wasn't a great deal, apart from the fact that her mother had a habit of dumping her with others.

After another minute or so of silence, while Georgie focused on keeping her mind open, Scott spoke. "Try something else."

Georgie put the doll down and reached towards the pile of Marylou's possessions, her hand hovering. She closed her eyes and waited a moment to see if one thing more than another appealed.

The shoes, she thought. Those little pink sneakers had probably taken Marylou to lots of different places. She had played games in them, visited friends in them, worn them to school.

Her fingers closed over the sparkly laces on one of the shoes, and she pulled it closer.

Immediately, Marylou's face blinked out, and in its place appeared a large, low building. At first, the perspective was from some distance away, but then suddenly it was up close, and Georgie was able to see that it was a school. The playground was full of children running, little feet flashing everywhere in all kinds of shoes.

"The shoes," she said, her voice catching. "They were the clue. When I picked up the shoe, I was thinking of Marylou wearing them to school—and look." She glanced up at Scott, her pulse beating faster. "Can you see it?"

His eyes were fixed on the crystal ball. "I can, yes. But is this her school back home, where she lived with her dad, or is it the school she's at now?"

"I don't know." Georgie stared at the scene intently, looking for something that might identify it. It looked like schools everywhere: lots of windows, wide steps up to the classrooms, trees, and a small playground area.

Playground, she thought. That seemed to be a common theme with Marylou. She focused on it, and as it grew larger, looked at each component. Play equipment varied a lot. There were slides, sometimes climbing nets, sometimes little mock shop fronts. Quickly, she imprinted the details on her mind; images could disappear as quickly as they appeared. "Playground equipment," she murmured to Scott. "Remember these things... red and blue sails for shade. There's a yellow climbing wall kind of setup, with all kinds of cutout shapes for fingers and feet. An open red slide and a kind of spiral pipe thingy that kids slide down too... That's in two shades of blue. There's something that looks like the prow of a ship, with a wheel... Oh no, it's *going*!"

The image dissolved into the first one she had

seen, a distant view of the school. Georgie caught a glimpse of a noticeboard near the front gate—the electronic kind that let you program in different events —but then that was gone too.

"Darn it." She sat back in frustration. "I wish you could just take a picture of what's in the crystal ball with your phone." Anticipating his question, she added, "Yes, I have tried, and no, it doesn't work."

"Hang on." Scott went over to the drawer where she kept pens and notepads and other assorted everyday items and brought a pen and paper back to the table. "Let's write that down while we remember. You said something like a ship, a ship's wheel, was it…?"

"Yes, and red and blue sails." He scribbled while they went over what she had seen.

"Tomorrow," Georgie suggested, "we can make a list of the schools in the area and drive around, see if we can see the right place. We'd be more likely to find Mary Lou—and her mother—at a school than that a commercial play center. She'll be at the school five days a week."

"Let's Google it first, have a look at the street view of the schools. You might be able to identify by doing that."

"Yes! Great idea. And tomorrow, let's go back to the play center, too—cover all the bases."

Scott pointed at the three remaining items: the sleepsuit, the party dress, and the old T-shirt belonging to her father that Marylou likes to wear to bed. "Want to do these now, or leave them for later?"

"I think we've got our best clue, but I can do those later tonight. The more information we have, the better." Georgie flicked the cover over the crystal ball. "We should go."

As she spoke, there was a sharp rap at the door, and a voice called: "Georgie? It's Jerry."

"Come in," she answered, then stood up and went over to the small counter area to pick up the dessert she had prepared for the communal supper. "Scott, can you take this? I've got a basket full of bread rolls to take as well."

Jerry stepped inside and closed the door behind him. "Got a minute?"

"Just barely," Georgie said. "I'm running late as it is." She turned and said teasingly, "And speaking of running late, I thought you had an intimate little dinner with Jaxx tonight?"

"No doubt the whole world knows about that," he said with an edge of irritation in his voice.

"Oh, they do," Georgie assured him. "Half the crowd here is fascinated, and half of them want to lynch you."

"Because of Tammy." His face was resigned.

"Pretty much. She's got a lot of friends here, Jerry."

"Just for the record," he told her, folding his arms and leaning back against the door, "this thing with

Jaxx tonight had nothing to do with me. Tammy and Jaxx set it up between them. And I'm doing Tammy a favor keeping Jaxx out of *your* hair."

"For tonight, anyway," Georgie said. Then her eyes lit up. "Can I use you tomorrow morning, too? I want to do some exploring in the local area, and the last thing I need is Jaxx tailing me again."

For a moment, Jerry said nothing, staring at her, then he said, "I'll help you if you help me."

Something about his voice made her take another look at him. He looked unusually tense.

"Look, just put down that basket for a moment." He jerked his head towards the table. "Can we sit down?"

This was not the Jerry she knew. Not Mr. Congeniality, who just seem to roll through life conning everyone in sight or winning them over with a smile and a warm glance.

Georgie put the basket back on the counter and nodded, sitting down. Jerry pushed himself off the door and sat down too.

"I'll leave you to it—take these things across, meet you over there," Scott said.

"No. Stay," Jerry said immediately.

"Jerry, you've almost got me worried," said Georgie. "What's going on?"

"It's Tammy." With great deliberation, Jerry linked his hands together on the table, the grip strong enough to make his knuckles white. "I've asked her to marry me, maybe a dozen times. She said no every time."

"And that surprises you?" Georgie couldn't help herself. "Think back, Jerry. You tried to pull a fast one when she was ready to set up the vintage section back at the RV empire, you keep running off to see Jaxx Saxby whenever she clicks her fingers…and knowing you, I'm sure there are a dozen more things that I have no clue about."

"I think you're letting our history as kids influence you too much, Georgie. I'm not that bad."

"The jury is out on that one, Jerry. Although," George conceded, "I must admit you have improved since Tammy came on the scene. *Slightly.*" She drilled him with a fierce stare. "But honestly, Jerry—Jaxx Saxby?"

Jerry thumped the table. "I am sick to death of hearing about Jaxx. It's business; I've said that all along. You *know* how vindictive she can be. With her influence on social media, she could do some real damage to the business if we offend her."

Georgie shook her head. She put both hands out to the sides, palms up, and pretended to weigh up alternatives. "Jaxx Saxby—Tammy Dyson. Gee, I wonder which one you should choose?"

Annoyance flared again in Jerry's eyes, but he bit back whatever he had been about to say, huffed out a sigh, and nodded. "Okay. You're right."

Georgie blinked at him. "I'm right? Did you just say I'm *right?*"

"Tonight, I'm going to tell Jaxx that if she has any further problems, we'll send out one of our senior mechanics."

Well. Jerry had managed to surprise her.

"Don't tell her tonight. Leave it for tomorrow," Georgie said. "Remember, we need you to keep her occupied tomorrow morning as well."

"That's right; you need a favor. Which brings me to what I want from you." He hitched his hips up a little off the seat so he could reach into the back pocket of his pants. He pulled out a small velvet bag with a gold insignia on the front, undid the tie, and withdrew a black box.

Georgie's mouth fell open. That box could only contain a ring. She looked up at Scott and was surprised to see a knowing grin on his face.

The rat. He had known all about this!

"Tomorrow night," Jerry said, opening the box, "I'm going to ask her *again*. In public. With the band playing one of her favorite numbers in the background." He swallowed hard and turned the box around so she could see the ring. "This is a ring she put on one of her Pinterest boards a few months ago, so I know it's right for her. When I saw the photo, I bought it right away, hid it away until now." He gave a twisted grin. "She's said 'no' three times since then. Nothing like living in hope, right?"

Georgie reached out and took the box from him, biting her lip to keep her emotions under control. "Jerry —"

"If you're going to say I don't deserve her, I know that," he said quickly. "But for Tams, I'll try. I'll never stop trying."

"Dammit," said Georgie. "Now you've made me cry."

Scott was already handing her a Kleenex.

"And," she said, "I wasn't going to say you don't deserve her, I was going to say it's gorgeous, and she'll love it to death."

"1940s. Vintage platinum and diamonds," Jerry said. "It's her. It's so totally her." He looked at her with a touch of hesitation. "So, what do you say? Can you help me set it up? Make it all just right?"

Georgie laughed, unable to control the faintly hysterical note to her voice. "Why not? Tammy will be so keyed up anticipating *Seth's* surprise proposal for Layla; she won't notice a thing."

Jerry stared at her. "*What?*"

"Oh, right, you wouldn't know." Georgie rolled her eyes. "There's something in the air. I've just been helping Seth choose a ring, ready to spring this on Layla tomorrow night. Now you." Immediately, she whipped around to shoot Scott a warning glance. "Don't even think about it."

He shrugged and said to Jerry, "I am going to

marry her one day. She just needs to get used to the idea."

Georgie sank back into her seat and closed her eyes for a second, wondering how she would manage to find a missing child, act as MC for a talent quest, keep Jaxx Saxby at bay as well as do a fake interview with her the next afternoon, *and* coordinate *two* surprise proposals.

Exactly when had all semblance of normality left her life?

CHAPTER 12

Searching for a School

The following day Georgie opened her eyes, then sighed and closed them again. She thought how nice it would be to stay in bed and rest for a week before finally forcing her lids open.

Busy day coming up.

She gave Scott a nudge. "Get up, sleepyhead."

Scott grunted, pulled the quilt up over his shoulders, and lay there unmoving.

"Scott." She shook him by the shoulder. "It's almost 9 o'clock. I should have been up hours ago."

A grunt of protest emerged from under the quilt, and a sleepy voice mumbled, "What's the rush? Sleep in."

"I wish." Georgie clambered over the top of him, hit the floor, and padded over to switch on the coffee machine. Caffeine. She needed coffee and something to eat. Why had she let Layla talk her into trying another glass of champagne? Oh, right, it just kind of went with the rest of the crazy evening. Talent quest followed by a sing-along followed by a jam session. At some point, she had given up worrying about what would happen tomorrow and just joined in the general festivities.

She reflected that the trouble with giving up was that you usually paid for it in the cold clear light of day.

On the table, her phone dinged. Georgie went across to pick it up, and as she did so, her eye fell on Marylou's Elsa doll.

Rosemary. She'd forgotten to get back to her. How could she have forgotten? After *promising* that she would phone and let her know, no matter how late it was.

She flipped open the cover of her phone and, as she had expected, it was a message from Rosemary. It simply said, "Any news?"

Just a gentle prod, Georgie thought, as she might expect from someone with Rosemary's innate good manners.

Behind her, she heard the sound of Scott's feet hitting the floor. "Do I smell coffee?"

"You do. Sit down, and I'll make you a cup." She looked up from the phone. "I forgot all about Rosemary last night. I told her that I'd phone no matter how late, let her know if I found anything."

"Well, you had a lot of things to think about."

Scott wandered over and wrapped his arms around her. "Layla's engagement. Tammy's engagement. And you did a great job as MC last night."

Georgie let the phone fall back onto the table. "Thanks. I'll phone, but…coffee first. When I'm feeling more like a normal person, and I can carry on a decent conversation, I'll phone her."

Scott yawned and scratched his chin. "Maybe hold off on that? Rather than get her hopes up again, wait until we've been back to the play center, tried to locate the school. Give her something a bit more concrete."

Georgie wavered for a moment. She really *would* prefer to just scout around with Scott, without Rosemary's hopeful face beside her.

"I could say I didn't have time last night," she said. "It's only half a fib because I didn't do a reading on *those*." She indicated the rest of the pile.

"You know how to do guilt better than almost anyone I know," Scott said. "Just tell her you got held up; you will do another reading today and call her back when you have news. That's all true."

She wavered, and then tiredness won out. "I guess I can live with that. Okay then – breakfast, see what Google can tell us about the schools, back to the play center, reconnoiter schools, do a final reading, phone Rosemary. Oh, and I have to do that fake interview with Jaxx in the afternoon and see the band about songs for Layla and Tammy." Her head already spinning, she went to grab a coffee. "Sounds like a plan."

Thanks to the wonders of Google Earth and school websites that were a mine of information about classrooms and playgrounds, Georgie finally tracked down a school that seemed right. There was an electronic board by the gate and photos on the website showing the installation of new playground equipment just fifteen months before.

"I think I found it," she said to Scott, punching the air. "Look at this. It really does exist."

"I don't know why you're surprised," he said. "Plenty of the things you've seen in the crystal ball checked out online. Like finding the preppers in Kentucky."

"Yes, but half of that was thanks to your mother," she reminded him. "She was the one who told us to look for a county in the center of the state. Maybe we should have called her in on this one too."

"She's all wrapped up in my new nephew at the moment," he said with a laugh. "If we get stuck, maybe we can give her a call."

"We'll try to leave her alone." Georgie crossed off "Google schools" on her list and ran a pencil down the rest of the items. "I want to go and try to catch the band before we head off – give them fair warning about what's coming up tonight. And swear them to secrecy. It's doing my head in, trying to keep things straight. I've let Layla into the secret about Tammy and Jerry, but nobody else, of course. And Tammy knows about Layla." She ticked off additional items on her fingers. "I've lined up Tammy to sing *Everybody Loves a Lover* just before Seth proposes, and I thought I'd get Tammy and Jerry to do *Ring of Fire* as a duet just after that…which I'll tell Tammy is an extra for Layla because she loves it almost as much as Tammy, but *Jerry* will know it's all for Tammy. Then Jerry can grab her by the hand and make his proposal." She looked at Scott, her brow furrowed. "Do you think that sounds alright?"

"I *think* I could almost follow that, but I don't know why you're asking me. I'm a mere male. It all sounds fine."

Dissatisfied, Georgie frowned at him. "Never mind, I'll just ask Tammy about Layla's, Layla about Tammy's, and try to stay sane."

She gathered up some playlists she had scribbled down and headed off out the door. "I'll get this organized with the band, and then we can leave. Oh, and as well, we need to pick up more champagne for Layla. More champagne all round, come to think about it. And wine." She groaned. "Much as I'm going to enjoy all this, I'll be glad to relax when it's over."

Forty-five minutes later, after making sure Jerry's diversionary tactics with Jaxx were working, Georgie and Scott headed out, GPS coordinates in place, to find Marylou's school. Or the one they thought was Marylou's school.

When they pulled up outside, Georgie instantly recognized the electronic noticeboard and the low-lying school buildings. "This is it. I *thought* it was, on Google, but now that I can see it in front of me, it looks exactly like the crystal ball showed it. Oh, man. My heart is jumping out of my chest."

"Hmm. Something is happening here today." Scott nodded at the cars in the school car park and the bumper-to-bumper parking outside. "Rehearsals? Fundraiser?"

Georgie looked at kids walking out holding balloons and family groups strolling around. She peered closer. "I can see some striped tents between those two buildings. Maybe they have a school market day?"

Scott pointed to the notice board. "There's your answer."

"Annual School Fair." Georgie read from the board. "Oh, wow." Her hand shot to her mouth. "How lucky can you get? They might not be here. They probably won't be here."

"Think positively. The crystal ball brought you

here, didn't it?" Scott opened the door and got out of his side of the car. "You might have more to report to Rosemary than you expected."

"And it won't look odd, our being here, with the Fair and all."

They made their way across the road and through the gates, hearing the sound of a school music group performing as they got closer to the tents. Many of the classrooms were open, showing tables stacked with baked goods for sale and unwanted toys recycled to raise funds. They could see tarps laid out on the ground for some trash and treasure stalls, plus the usual fair attractions—mini-golf, ring toss, and a dozen more.

"Over there," Georgie said, pointing. "I have to have a look at the dinnerware. An impromptu engagement present for Layla and Tammy."

Scott looked at her. "You've got to be kidding. Those two have more dinnerware than Wal-Mart."

Georgie spared him a pitying glance. "Not the same thing. Just humor me, Scott."

He held up both hands in front of him. "Saying nothing. Just tagging along."

She made a beeline for the table of retro dinnerware – half of which, she had to admit, was junk – and found two half-decent sets and one that was missing a cup and saucer but was otherwise perfect for her own trailer. "Before you start counting," she told Scott firmly, "one of these is for me."

"Saying nothing," he muttered again and took the bags from her. "You Jane, me packhorse."

"I think you're getting the jungle and the Wild West mixed up," she told him, "but I appreciate the sentiment." Then she stopped dead and flung back an arm to stop him. "Stop."

"Oof," he said, rubbing his stomach. "What do you want to buy now?"

She half-turned and grabbed him by the elbow. "It's them. Oh my goodness. Don't look now—wait, yes, do look but don't make it obvious. Over there by the ring toss, standing near the school mascot. I'm sure that's Marylou."

Scott had studied the photos as much as she had. He stole a glance in the direction she indicated, and his eyebrows flew up.

"I think you're right. It is."

"Look at the man with them. I'm sure that must be him, the one I saw in the crystal ball." Georgie was standing at an angle, looking without appearing to. "He's the right build, tall and thickset. I have to get a closer look."

"They don't know you," Scott reminded her. "Go and stand in line as though you're waiting for a turn at the ring toss."

"I'll try to get a photo. Come with me; you can pose with the school mascot so that I can get them in the background."

"Pose with a bear? I *think* it's a bear. The things I

do." Nevertheless, Scott walked over towards the ring toss.

Well done, she thought when he exchanged a few laughing words with the mascot and skillfully turned him towards the camera so that the ring toss competition was visible to one side. She tapped the phone a couple of times and gave him a thumbs-up.

"Here," she said, showing him the results while keeping one eye on Marylou and her mother. She swiped at the screen to enlarge the photo and zoomed in. "It is, isn't it? It *is* her."

Scott nodded. "Unless she has a twin."

Georgie sneaked another look at the threesome: Paige, Marylou, and the unknown man. Paige looked a little nervy and thinner than in the photos Georgie had seen. The man with her bent down to say something close to her ear and put a hand on her back, urging her along. She nodded and turned to call to her daughter.

"Emmylou! Time to go!"

Georgie clutched Scott's arm. "Did you hear that? *Emmylou.* Close enough so the kid will answer to it. Scott, they're leaving! What do we do? I don't know what to do."

They stared at each other for a few seconds and then said at the same time, "Follow them."

Finding out where Paige and Marylou lived would be the best possible information they could take back to Rosemary.

CHAPTER 13

Jaxx Delivers a Surprise

Georgie dropped Scott off at his truck camper, waiting while he unloaded a plentiful supply of champagne, wine, and soda, and gave him a list of instructions to follow for other things that needed doing.

"I had no idea that these things took so much organization," he said good-naturedly, reaching for the bags from the school fair.

She stopped him. "Leave those. I need to wrap them, think of a suitable message to go with both. Can you check on both Seth and Jerry? Seth will be a nervous wreck. Jerry is usually cool, but I don't know…he seemed a bit different this morning."

"He'll probably need a beer after a morning with Jaxx," Scott predicted. He leaned a forearm on the open window. "What are you going to say to Rosemary?"

"I'll tell her that I got nothing on the doll. I'll do a quick reading on the other things; there might be something vague I can pass on." Georgie thought for a moment. "I can tell her that I caught a quick glimpse of a school in the crystal ball, so I'm sure Marylou must go to school around here somewhere. That will do."

After following Paige and Marylou to a small, neat house in the outer suburbs, Georgie and Scott discussed how much to tell Rosemary until Marylou's father arrived. Georgie liked Rosemary, but the other woman was so keen to have a happy outcome for Shelton that she might take it into her head to go out to Paige's house and see for herself—and maybe make it too apparent that she was watching. What if Paige, or the man with them, saw her?

What if they ran? What if there was violence? The man with Paige looked big and strong.

In the end, they had decided it might be best to wait for Shelton and let him set things up with the local police or a lawyer or whatever.

"Good luck." Scott winked. "See you over at the Big Event."

She looked at him suspiciously. "There's not going to be *three* engagements tonight, Scott."

"Of course not," he said, all innocence. "Might be only one, depending on Tammy's reaction."

"You know what? I think it will all depend on how Jerry phrases it. If ever Mr. Silvertongue needed to call on all his skills, it'll be tonight. Anyway," Georgie started to move away, "It's sure to be entertaining."

Lunch was a smoothie made of fruit and ice cream, and then Georgie wrapped the retro dinnerware she'd found. She'd find a proper engagement present for both later, but for now, they'd be thrilled.

As long as Tammy said yes, of course.

But she knew Jerry. If it were a no' that would make him more determined than ever. Even if it took years.

Then, as though she had summoned him just by thinking about him, Jerry phoned.

"Hi there," she greeted him cheerfully. "How are the nerves?"

"I'll be fine," he said, but she noticed that his voice was a tad higher and faster than usual. "Georgie, I'm over here with Jaxx."

She looked at the clock on the wall. "Still?"

"She was telling me an interesting story," he said. "Apparently, she met a new client of yours the other day."

In the background, she heard Jaxx's voice prompting him. "*Rosemary.*"

"Rosemary," he repeated. "Jaxx says she had a coffee with you, heard Rosemary's story."

Jerry already knew that; it was the whole reason

she'd given him the task of keeping Jaxx away from them. So, he hadn't let on to Jaxx that he knew.

"Yes…?"

"She got her researcher on the job, told him to find out the facts in the background."

A wave of anger swept through her. "So much for Jaxx's word." She raised her voice. "Are you there, Jaxx? You promised you'd hold off if I did the interview!"

Jaxx took the phone. "Calm down. I'm not *doing* anything. I just needed to see if this thing had legs. I gave my researcher the name, the Facebook page, a few details."

Still steamed, Georgie snapped, "Well, we can forget the interview, then."

"*Georgie.* I'm doing you a *favor* here. I'm not calling Rosemary, not taking it further, and I *should*. There's a story here. More than you *know*."

Georgie went cold. "What do you mean?"

"This Facebook page, it's brand new. Shelton Crest doesn't exist. Not surprising, with a name like that. Sounds more like a hotel than a person."

"What about Rosemary?"

"Rosemary Scully? She seems to check out. Her Facebook page is like anyone else's, except she doesn't have any photos of herself with Shelton. That's a bit weird. She talks about him a lot, where they go, what they do. Nothing about any daughter, though."

Georgie clutched the phone harder. "So what are you telling me?"

"My researcher says that abusive husbands have caught onto this Facebook thing to track down a wife on the run—even in protective custody. The 'missing child' thing has had a few bad outcomes. People try to help, share the photo, "have you seen this child?" The husband follows up, finds the kid, and bingo."

"Are you sure that this is one of those cases?"

"No." Jaxx was starting to sound bored. "Just telling you what it looks like. He started up the page out of nowhere, and he's not showing up anywhere else. He's like a ghost." Her voice changed as though she'd turned away from the phone. "There. I told her. Now *you* owe me, Jerry."

The suggestive purr in her voice made Georgie sick. *Leave him alone*, she felt like saying, picturing Tammy's face.

But then, it was up to Jerry to tell Jaxx to take a hike. He was a grown man.

"Georgie?" Jerry was back.

"A bit longer," she said, knowing he'd know what she meant. "I'll do some checking. And—thanks."

"I look forward to tonight," he said, his meaning clear. "We quits now?"

"We're quits."

She put down the phone.

Nothing was ever simple, was it?

Was Shelton who he said he was? Just a quiet man

who didn't like social media unless it helped him get his daughter back?

Or was he a predator?

Her eye fell on the BEST DAD EVER t-shirt—Marylou's father's t-shirt; the one she sometimes slept in.

Shelton had once worn it.

Marylou's shoes had led her to the little girl. Could this t-shirt tell her something about its owner?

She sat down with the crystal ball and picked up the t-shirt, slowly shaking it out of its folds. It smelled of bubblegum and hair shampoo—Marylou's little-girl scent.

With one hand on the t-shirt, she walked her fingers over the surface of the crystal ball and then imagined Marylou going to sleep in the shirt, hugging her Elsa doll.

Then she imagined the little girl's father wearing it before passing it on to Marylou.

It didn't take long. The mist in the center of the crystal ball swirled and turned dark grey, as it had several times before showing people who wished others harm.

There was a face in the mist, but it was indistinct. A shadowy figure: the face wasn't clear, as it had been in the photo of Marylou and her dad on the waterslide.

Then it swept over her, a wash of ill-feeling and hidden malice: an unmistakable threat to Marylou and her mother. Her mind filled with the understanding of what had happened.

There had been no neglectful mother; there was no child at risk. Not from Paige. The only danger to Paige and Marylou was from the man who was hunting them.

He was using Rosemary as his tool—and through her, Georgie.

She pushed the t-shirt away, sick to her stomach. It had been so close. So close.

She had almost delivered Marylou to the enemy.

Georgie forced herself to call Rosemary. None of this was her fault. All too soon, the poor woman was going to be the recipient of some horrible news.

She probably wouldn't believe it at first. If Shelton had been cunning enough to pull this off so far, he was smart enough to continue playing the part with Rosemary as long as he had to.

Rosemary picked up on the first ring. "Georgie! So glad to hear from you. I've been dying to hear. How did you go? Any more news?"

"Hi, Rosemary." Georgie made her voice cheerful and faintly embarrassed. "I'm sorry I've taken so long to get back to you. Things are incredibly hectic here. I've just got a tiny window of time now—but I'll catch up with you properly tomorrow or the day after."

"So, nothing?" The hope in Rosemary's voice was fading.

"I got a very quick image of a school. I'm sure she's going to school around here somewhere—but I think on the very edge of the county, probably inland rather than near the ocean." It made her feel better to hand out a little bit of misdirection.

"Oh." Rosemary cheered up immediately. "I can tell Shelton that. His PI can get onto it; check out the schools over that way."

Georgie very much doubted that there had ever been any PI—much less discussions with the police about a missing daughter.

"When did you say Shelton is coming?" she asked.

"He's going to try to make it tomorrow. If not, the day after. He's been held up a bit."

At Rosemary's words, a wave of dread surged through Georgie. Suddenly, she sensed that Shelton Crest had not been held up at all. He was somewhere close by, right now.

Maybe even watching her, to see where she went.

She swallowed hard. "Okay. That's good if he's not ready yet. I'm going to be busy for the rest of today, and probably tomorrow too. Perhaps we could meet up on Tuesday morning? First thing?"

"I'll suggest it," Rosemary agreed enthusiastically. "He'll be thrilled."

"Great. I'll be in touch. Hang in there, Rosemary."

Georgie ended the call and immediately went to the Facebook page that Shelton had set up, intending to take a screen capture of the photo of Shelton with Marylou at the water park.

The page was no longer available.

CHAPTER 14

Warning the Victim

Just to be on the safe side, Georgie borrowed Seth's hire car to go and see Paige and Marylou. Her truck was far too distinctive, and Seth's car had nice dark tinted windows. Nevertheless, she checked her mirrors constantly. She'd never forgive herself if she led Shelton to Paige and little Marylou.

The thickset man she'd seen first in the crystal ball and then at the school fair answered the door.

Up close, his face wasn't threatening but calm. He looked at her, and then behind her, and waited for Georgie to speak first.

"Hi." She smiled, wishing her voice didn't sound quite so hesitant. "My name's Georgie Goode. I wondered if I might speak to…" she stopped briefly, wondering if Paige was still Paige. "The lady of the house?"

His eyes grew more watchful. "May I ask what it's about?"

She hadn't thought past this point. She hadn't even thought *up* to this point.

Then she remembered what she had heard Paige call her daughter. "It's about Emmylou," she said. "I'm from the school."

Which was kind of true.

Expressionless, he looked at her for a good few seconds before finally nodding. "One moment." He stepped back from the front door, turned toward the back of the house, and called, "Sage! Someone from the school for you."

Very cautious, she thought. He wasn't going to let her through the front door without knowing more. So it was 'Sage'. Clever. That would sound enough like "Paige" to make her turn around if someone called her name.

Paige came to the door.

"Hello, Sage," Georgie said. "I wonder if I might have a moment of your time to talk about Emmylou?"

Paige glanced up at the man standing beside her and then back at Georgie. "I'm sorry, do I know you?"

Georgie threw caution to the winds. "No, but we've had word that someone has been asking around about Emmylou. Except they called her 'Marylou'. I thought you should know."

The blood drained from Paige's face, and she clutched at the man's arm. "Sam!"

He wrapped an arm around her shoulders, supporting her, and finally opened the door. "You'd better come in."

In the short distance between the front door and the living room, Georgie decided to come clean immediately. They needed to know.

"In here," said Sam, steering her past the family room, where Marylou was watching cartoons, into a slightly more formal area for adults.

She sat in the chair he indicated, and the two of them sat opposite, on a two-seater sofa. Paige's eyes were wide and fearful.

"Please hear me out," Georgie said quickly. "This will all sound crazy, but I want to help you." She opened the bag she'd brought with her and tipped the contents out on the floor: the Elsa doll, the sleepsuit, the party dress, the shoes, and lastly, the t-shirt. Paige's eyes fixed on that immediately, and if anything, she went even paler.

"First," Georgie said, "He doesn't know where you are. That's why I'm here, to warn you. May I tell you the whole story?"

Paige nodded mutely, biting her lip, thrusting her hands between her knees to keep them from trembling.

It took only a few minutes to outline it all, from Rosemary's first visit to the revelations about the Facebook page. "I'm assuming you were not a neglectful mother," Georgie finished, "and that you didn't run away with Marylou."

Sam answered for her, rubbing his hand comfortingly on her knee. "You assume right."

"And the story Rosemary heard from Shelton, about you driving off listening to *Good Vibrations*? No truth in that?"

"Of course not," said Paige angrily. "And his name isn't Shelton Crest. It's Dave Palfrey. *And* I bet anything you like; there's no PI involved—just Dave."

Georgie nodded. "I feel Rosemary is the innocent in all this. I think she's a good person."

"I imagine she would be," Paige said bitterly. "That's how he operates. He'll use her until he finds us and then toss her aside. She would never know what happened to him."

"I also have a strong feeling that he's here now, somewhere in the area," Georgie told them. "I don't know for sure, but I'm not usually wrong about these things."

"He's not supposed to come anywhere near us," Paige said. She looked at Sam, hope in her eyes. "You can get him now, can't you?"

The curiosity obviously showed on Georgie's face because Sam gave Paige's knee a quick pat and explained, "I'm with the police. I can take care of it now."

A huge weight fell from Georgie's shoulders. "Thank goodness. I didn't know what to do. Didn't know whether to contact the police or come and warn you, but—"

She sent a quick apologetic glance at Sam. "No offense, but I didn't know how quickly the police here would act, or even *if* they would. So I thought, Paige first."

"Good decision. You weren't to know."

"Well. I'll leave it all up to you, then." She added, looking at Sam, "I borrowed a car to drive here, a hire car. I don't think anyone followed me."

"He won't get past me," Sam said. "Don't worry. And thanks."

Georgie took out one of her cards and handed it to Sam. She caught the quirk of his lips as he looked at it: Georgie B. Goode, 8th Generation Gypsy Fortune Teller.

Grinning cheerfully at him, she said, "Don't worry. I don't think you'll need my services. But I'd like to know how it all turns out if you wouldn't mind."

"I'll do that."

They walked her to the door, and Paige gave her a quick hug. "Thank you. *Thank you.* This could have all turned out so differently."

"My pleasure." Georgie shook hands with them both. "I feel sorry for Rosemary, but she needs to know."

By the time she reached the car, her mind was already turning to engagement parties.

She so much wanted Tammy to be the sister she'd never had. And *she* could be the sister Tammy had never had.

Please say yes, Tammy, she thought.

Because she did think that Jerry might be changing at last.

What did you wear to a double engagement party? Or a double engagement party that still might turn into a single engagement if Tammy said no?

60s beach party clothes, she decided. For tonight, she'd leave her BoHo and gypsy wardrobe behind, even if she did love it all. Tonight was about Layla and Tammy, the retro queens, and she would dress for the occasion. Vintage clothes, vintage engagement rings, and lots of love and laughter and celebration.

Besides, she liked a change every so often.

Bermuda shorts and cotton top, or A-line mini-dress?

A-line floral print mini-dress, she decided. Dress up—in a manner of speaking—for the engagement party. Besides, she liked the fresh citrus green and yellow of the background with hot pink blooms.

Time to party!

CHAPTER 15

The Big Question

Seth looked just fine until Tammy walked over to give him the signal. Immediately, he cast a panicked look at Georgie and swallowed hard.

"Go on," she said, pushing him toward Tammy. "Go."

Watching them walk away, Tammy chatting gaily to distract him while she waved Layla over to join him, Georgie clutched Scott. "I'm going to cry. This is too romantic for words."

"And you wouldn't let me follow the trend," he said with pretended despondency. "It's not too late. I *am* going to marry you one day, you know."

That made her laugh, as he knew it would. Like her, he knew that it would happen when the time was right. She had a sneaking feeling that might be after she had met his family.

"Come on," he said, urging her forward. "We need a front-row view for this!"

Tammy, looking fabulous as always in pale mauve Bermuda shorts and a fitted striped top with a narrow belt, ran up the two steps to the stage area and took the mic. "I know it's a Beach Party theme," she announced to the crowd, "but I just can't resist the chance to sing one of my all-time favorites." She waved at a lot of the younger retro set who were there as couples. "Here's a chance to recover from the Swim and the Stomp—before we start the next round!"

As always, she was greeted with cheers and whistles.

"Ladies and gentleman…this song was made popular by Doris Day in 1958 and then re-released by the Shirelles in 1963. So it fits our 60s rally perfectly!"

More cheers. "It's also a favorite song of my good friend Layla, so… Layla?" She beckoned with a laugh. "Want to come up and join me in the last verse?"

Standing in the front row with Seth, Layla laughed. "Tammy, no! You're the one with the set of pipes."

Now right behind them, scarcely able to contain herself with excitement, Georgie gave her a good-natured push. "Go on! You can *more* than hold a tune.

It's party time!" She winked at Seth. "Seth will be right here cheering you on."

"Sure will." He cast her one last desperate glance. "I'll wait for you at the bottom of the steps. Come on."

"Whoa, nicely done," Scott said, watching them move away. "You women are a devious bunch."

"Sssh. Have you got a Kleenex?" Georgie was already dabbing at the corners of her eyes, and Tammy hadn't even started singing yet.

"Men don't carry Kleenex," Scott said, handing her a paper napkin that had held his hamburger. "It's got ketchup on it. Sorry."

With Layla beside her, Tammy started to sing, her voice low on the opening phrase. "*Everybody…loves a lover…*"

Throughout the song, she encouraged Layla to join in and let her finish alone on *"Fell in love with you…"*

Layla took a sweeping bow and prepared to leave the stage, but Tammy held her back. "One more thing."

"No, no more." Layla made dissenting motions and backed away. "Over to you."

"No," Tammy said. "Over to Seth."

She stepped back out of the way and let Seth take her place, handing him the microphone.

Layla looked puzzled, and then comprehension grew as Seth reached into his pocket and took out the box containing the ring. As she eyed the small velvet box, her hand flew to her mouth.

Seth took the mic that Tammy handed him, gaining confidence as he looked into Layla's astonished face. "Layla," he said, smiling at her as he spoke, "We've known each other now for—what, about six months? In that time, I've come to know what a fine person you are. You're fun, and caring, and…" he stood back and cast an admiring glance at her bright 60s beach outfit, "you wear the *best* clothes."

That one got a cheer from the grinning crowd, watching and listening to the drama unfold. Layla waved at them and then looked back at Seth, her hand pressed to her chest.

Seth finally relaxed. He winked at the audience and looked around for Tammy, handing her the mic and the ring box so he could take Layla's hand in his. Tammy grinned at the audience and held the mic close so nobody would miss a word.

"Layla," Seth said, going down smoothly on one knee, "There's nothing I want more than to share the rest of my life with you. Will you marry me?" He smiled at her and held up the ring, glinting a beautiful rose gold in the stage lights.

Speechless, she nodded, barely holding back the tears, and let him slip the ring onto her finger.

The crowd erupted. Seth stood, lifted Layla in his arms, kissed her, and whirled her around, relieved that it was over, clearly thrilled by Layla's reaction and now playing to the crowd.

Georgie gulped back happy tears and clutched Scott harder. "Omigod."

"And now," Scott said, handing her a torn-off square of paper toweling, "for Part Two."

Georgie hiccupped and scrubbed at her eyes. "Oh, man."

Tammy took the mic back and grinned at the crowd. "It's true, isn't it, folks? Everybody does indeed love a lover! But before we let them go, Jerry and I are going to do another one of Layla's favorites—which also happens to be one of ours. It seems to fit the occasion."

The band started up the first chords to *Ring of Fire*, and Jerry began to sing. He had an excellent deep baritone that suited the number, and he and Tammy had gone through it twice that afternoon, using Johnny Cash and June Carter on stage in *Walk the Line* for inspiration.

Naturally, Tammy had no idea of what was coming at the end of it.

While Seth hugged Layla close, grinning at each other and softly joining in some of the chorus, the crowd cheered and sang the chorus: *Ring of fire! RING OF FIRE!"*

After a resounding ovation, Jerry took the mic. Layla beamed at Georgie, her face incandescent with joy. Not only was she about to watch her best pal's marriage proposal, but she was also engaged herself. Georgie could only begin to imagine how she felt.

"That was a special presentation for our good friends, Seth and Layla, on the night of their engagement," Jerry said and waited while the inevitable round of cheering stopped.

"But," he said, "I have one more thing to say."

Layla glanced up at Seth in anticipation, her eyes shining, and Georgie saw him squeeze her hand. He still thought it was all about them, but Layla knew differently.

"What most of you don't know," Jerry said, "is that I've asked Tammy here to marry me—oh, at least a dozen times, would it be, Tammy?"

Narrowing her eyes at him, she spoke into her mic. "At least, Jerry, at least." Looking out at the spectators and grinning widely, she declared, "Maybe two dozen!"

"Well, every time, folks, Tammy has said a big NO. And I can understand why; I needed some taming first. But I figured, tonight, she might get carried away by all the romance in the air and agree to marry me, too. So…"

Jerry didn't get down on one knee. Instead, he ran a hand gently over Tammy's cheek and tilted her chin so he could look directly into her eyes. "Tammy, I'm hoping you won't say 'no' again. My life has taken on new meaning with you in it—and I promise I'll keep trying to please you until the day I die." He stroked her lips with his thumb and then looked out at the onlookers with a wry grin. "And even then, I'll probably *still* be trying to do what this girl wants!"

He looked back at Tammy, and his face grew serious. He let go of her and dipped into his pocket for the beautiful vintage ring, holding it up so that it glittered in the lights around the stage. "Tammy. Please. Make us both happy for the rest of our lives. Marry me."

She stood very still and looked at him and then took the hand that held out the ring, her fingers closing over his.

Georgie held her breath. Beside her, she could feel that even Scott was tense.

The crowd was silent.

"Jerry, I…" Tammy stretched up and kissed Jerry gently on the lips and then leaned back. "This is a big step. I'm going to have to think about it a bit more…"

Jerry leaned forward and whispered something in her ear. Then he whispered some more.

Tammy shook her head and looked at him. Even from where Georgie stood, you could see the sheen of tears in her eyes.

"Oh no," Georgie said. "No, Tammy, don't…"

Tammy looked at her feet and back at the band. Ready to come to the rescue with some upbeat music, they shifted their guitars.

She looked back at Jerry, her head on the side, and

then sent him a smile of such brilliance that it made the whole night light up.

"Okay, I've thought about it. I'll marry you."

Jerry punched the air, grabbed her hand, and slid the ring onto her finger before bending her backward in the dramatic kiss that the audience was waiting for.

Georgie shrieked and flung her arms around Scott, making him laugh as he staggered to keep his balance. Layla punched the air, and she and Seth moved in for a group hug.

The crowd went wild, and the band launched into *Good Vibrations*.

Georgie laughed, wiping her eyes. "There you go. I knew it as soon as I heard it, the day we got here. This place has good vibes."

CHAPTER 16

Good Vibrations

Just after five o'clock the next afternoon, Georgie saw Scott off to one of the local bars with Seth and Jerry and made her way towards where Tammy and Layla were waiting for her. They were in the same spot overlooking the beach as they'd been when Jaxx Saxby first turned up.

This time, there was no Jaxx to worry about. Incensed that Jerry had publicly chosen Tammy over her, she had huffily taken her entourage to a different RV park. Except for Seth, who had handed in his notice and told her that if she wanted him to finish the current shoot, she had better leave him alone for the rest of the day.

Jaxx had made a point of coming to see Georgie before she left.

"I just want you to know," she said, folding her arms and narrowing her eyes, "that I'm not going to leave that Rosemary Scully case alone. You never *did* come and do that on-camera interview you promised."

"That's because you broke your word and started digging into it after you agreed to leave it alone," Georgie told her, narrowing her eyes right back. "You can't have it both ways, Jaxx."

"I helped you solve the case."

"You almost put your foot in it first. You just don't know where to draw the line." Georgie, impatient with the other woman's histrionics, kept going. "I think it's best if we don't keep working together. Besides, you're a good enough investigator to do it yourself. You don't need me."

Looking startled at hearing praise from Georgie, Jaxx blinked. "You think so?"

"Yes." And really, Georgie did. Sure, she had helped Jaxx with some insights that the average person didn't have, but Jaxx did excel at investigation.

She just didn't have any people skills.

"Just one thing," Georgie said. "Leave it for a few days before you follow up, could you?"

"Why?" Jaxx demanded.

Georgie hesitated. "Let's just say that it would be best for little Marylou. Please?"

Jaxx stared at her, thinking. "If you agree to come with me to the haunted house. Just once."

"No."

"No filming. Just talk to me. Tell me what you pick up."

Georgie thought it over and finally sighed and nodded. If it would help Paige and Marylou... "As long as Seth is there when I'm doing it."

Jaxx shook her head, giving a wry smile. "So that you can be sure that we're not secretly filming?"

"Or recording it," Georgie agreed.

"Okay. Done. I'll be in touch." With that, Jaxx flounced off.

That little confrontation had been mid-morning. The next few hours had passed in a happy buzz of ongoing congratulations and celebrations, with Tammy and Layla in a huddle over vintage wedding dresses and retro wedding receptions – when they were not comparing and exclaiming over rings.

At twenty after three, Georgie got a call from Sam.

"It's done," he said in his calm, sure voice. "We've picked up Dave Palfrey, aka Shelton Crest. And we've talked to Rosemary Scully."

"Poor Rosemary," Georgie said, her heart constricting. "How's she taking it?"

"She wasn't willing to believe it at first, as you can imagine. But Paige talked to her—Paige and Marylou together. There were things…well, she's been able to fill in a few gaps. Her world has kind of fallen apart."

"Where is she now?"

"Back at the hotel, packing to catch a flight out. We'll be talking with her again."

"Well, I'm glad it worked out. Give my regards to Paige and Marylou." Georgie blew out a breath. "That was such a close call. I would never have forgiven myself if I'd fallen for his story and given Rosemary your address."

"She would never have forgiven herself either; now she knows what Paige and Marylou went through. Anyway. All's well that ends well."

"Thanks, Sam."

She ended the call and then gathered up her courage to make the final call.

Rosemary.

When Georgie finally reached their camp chairs, Tammy and Layla were—once again—admiring each other's rings. Tammy was showing Layla her Pinterest board, *THINGS I LOVE*, with the photo of the ring.

"I can't believe he *ordered* it. All that time ago!" Layla exclaimed, admiring it and comparing the photo to the real thing on Tammy's finger. "And hung on to it, through *three* more NOs."

"That just goes to show," Georgie said, sitting down, "that our Jerry really might be a reformed character."

Tammy grinned at her and held out her hand. "Have you seen my ring lately?"

Georgie gave a mock groan. "Not in the past five minutes, no. But I'll look again." She laughed at Tammy's besotted expression. "It *is* a gorgeous ring. I could look at it all day."

"So could I," Tammy said, holding it up to the sun, now getting lower in the sky, and watching it sparkle. "In fact, I do."

"As do I," said Layla, waving her hand around up near Tammy's. "Look, Georgie. Rose gold. Gorgeous."

"It is. Seth has good taste."

"He told me you went with him."

"Yes, but he chose it. Really, he did. I just approved it."

Tammy laid her hand in her lap and got serious. "Enough about us. How's Rosemary?"

"Devastated. Unbelieving. Well, she does *believe* it, but she's having a hard time adjusting. One minute she was looking forward to a happy future with a gorgeous little girl, and the next, she learned she'd been aiding and abetting an abusive husband. You can imagine."

"Yes." Tammy nodded soberly. "I *can* imagine—a wolf in sheep's clothing. Well, look what happened to Miss Molly. Same kind of deal."

It was, Georgie thought. Abuse of trust was always a bitter pill to swallow.

Tammy had had her share of it in her life, too. No wonder she had needed to be sure of Jerry.

Jerry and Tammy. The thought had Georgie beaming at her again. "You're going to be my sister-in-law. I'm so happy. I never thought Jerry would choose anybody I'd like."

"And I have decided," Layla said, "You are both going to be my honorary sisters-in-law, even if you aren't. So there."

"Done," said Georgie and Tammy together.

"There's just one thing I've got to know," Layla said, looking at Tammy, "unless it's private. In which case you don't have to tell me. But I'd love to know."

"I know what you're going to ask," said Tammy, with a tiny smile. "I thought you'd get around to it. I know you two too well."

She was correct; they did know each other that well—which is why Georgie knew precisely what was in Layla's mind. She nodded at her and turned to Tammy. "What *did* Jerry whisper in your ear?"

Layla cupped her ear and leaned closer to Tammy, her eyebrows arched. "Spill!"

Tammy's smile grew. "He just said that he had told Jaxx he wouldn't be available next time she called. Told her he was mine. *Mine.*"

Georgie and Layla both heaved satisfied sighs. "About time," they said in unison.

"And that he'd say the same to anyone else, anytime."

"Wow," Georgie said. "He *has* changed."

"Mind you," Tammy said, "I don't expect miracles. Jerry's Jerry. But he loves me, and I kinda like a challenge." She was silent for a moment. "He's got a good heart."

"That's what Grandma Rosa always said," Georgie told her, leaning across and giving her a one-armed hug. "She'll be so thrilled by this news."

"She was," Tammy said, laughing. "She was waiting for the phone call. Said she didn't need any crystal ball to see what was in the wind."

They all sat and watched the sun go down, listening to the band start up again in the background for the last night before they left.

Georgie waited, smiling in anticipation while she poured the wine. She had stopped and had a word to the band on the way over, so she knew what was coming.

"There you go," she said, raising her glass to her sister-in-law and honorary sister-in-law, as *Good Vibrations* began to play. "I told you that this place had good vibes. To us!"

"To us," they echoed.

A NOTE FROM THE AUTHOR

Well, that brings us to the end of the ninth book in the Georgie B. Goode Gypsy Trailer Mystery series! In this book, I deliberately threw a lot at Georgie so she'd be kept on her toes trying to juggle two different family secrets as well as her latest mystery! This story was a lot of fun to write, so I hope you had just as much fun reading it. If so, I'd really appreciate it if you would give a few minutes of your time and leave an honest review. Reviews really help a book to find an audience, and they help other readers to decide what they'd like to read, too!

There's just one more book to go to wrap up Series 1 of the 'Georgie' stories: *A Rocking Good Christmas!* Georgie is on her way home for Christmas when she stops for a hitch-hiker—an extremely disgruntled-looking Santa Claus. That turns out to be one of the worst decisions of her life…

I've provided you with a sample chapter to get a taste of what is to come!

Here's an invitation for you: subscribe to my newsletter to get news of new releases, bonus books, specials and a sneak peek at scenes from my books in progress. As a welcome gift, you'll also receive a copy of *Fortune's Wheel*, the prequel to the Georgie series.

Here's your chance to find out more about the intriguing old woman that Georgie sees as a kind of taciturn genie. Whether she wanted to believe it or not, from birth Georgie was destined to follow in Great-Grandma Rosa's footsteps—as well as inherit her crystal ball!

If you haven't already done so, visit my website below to join other readers and download your copy.

MargMcAlister.com/free-georgie-book/

ABOUT THE AUTHOR

Marg McAlister is the author of the popular Georgie B. Goode Cozy Mystery series (set in the USA) and Series 2 (Australian RV Adventure series), also featuring Georgie.

Marg lives by the sea on the mid-north coast of NSW, but she and her husband spend part of the year on The Gemfields in Central Queensland, living off the grid on their mining claim. While her husband digs for sapphires and zircons, operates the wash plant and drives around dirt tracks, Marg is usually writing —or socializing!

Marg is also the author of a series of books for aspiring writers, and the owner of Blue Gem Publishing, which publishes books in a range of genres.

Next in This Series
A ROCKING GOOD CHRISTMAS

Chapter 1

The last thing Georgie expected to see as she rounded a curve on the I-80 was Santa Claus, standing by the side of the road with his thumb out.

He even, she noted incredulously, had a bright red sack beside him, resting against a milepost.

Her first thought was, *You've got to be kidding me.*

Her second thought was, *This is a ploy.* She could still hear her father's voice from way back in her teen years when she first got her license: *"Number one rule, Georgina Bridget Goode, is NEVER STOP FOR HITCHHIKERS."*

She swiftly assessed the scene while slowing down a little. There was no broken-down car on the side of the road—or a broken-down sleigh, for that matter.

Not a reindeer in sight.

Curiouser and curiouser.

No bushes for a partner in crime to pop out of with a gun, either, which was a plus.

Georgie cruised past him, watching in her rear vision mirror, and he dropped his thumb, looked after her for a beat or two, and then turned away to wait for the next vehicle.

Probably, he wasn't surprised that a quaint, old-fashioned gypsy trailer hadn't stopped for him—especially if he had noticed there was a woman at the wheel of the truck towing it. He might even have guessed it was a woman whose father had drummed into her that she should never stop for hitchhikers.

Looking at his diminishing figure in the mirror, she slowed a little more. Her intuition wasn't sounding any warnings, and she wanted to know *why* Santa had to hitchhike.

Georgie hit the brakes and pulled over. The sun had already dropped below the horizon, and soon it would be dark. It would become more problematic for him to score a lift, and she was only a few miles away from the friendly little RV park where she was spending the night. He could get help there or find another ride. Or even stay in one of the cabins.

She saw, in her side mirror, the moment he realized that she had stopped. He picked up his sack, heaved it over his shoulder, and set off toward her with a shuffling run.

He was the right shape for a Santa Claus, but not the right shape to run very far or very fast.

Georgie picked up her phone and called Scott. He didn't answer, so she phoned Tammy.

"Georgie!" Tammy's voice bubbled through the phone. "I've been waiting to hear from you. Where are you?"

"I'm overnighting at Lucky Luke's, just east of North Platte," Georgie told her, with one eye on the mirror. "Almost there, but I'm picking up a hitchhiker. Just thought you should know in case my body is found on the side of the road any time soon."

"Are you *nuts?* Unless it's Mother Teresa…" Tammy's voice grew fainter for a moment as she turned away from the phone. "Jerry! Georgie said she's picking up a hitchhiker."

Her brother came onto the phone immediately. "Georgie, no. Drive on. Let someone else pick him up. Or them."

"It's all right," Georgie said. "It's Santa Claus. Hang on."

A red face, puffing from the run, appeared at her passenger-side window. His beard, she saw immediately, was real. His eyebrows were snowy and bushy. Sweat ran down from the snow-white band on the edge of his red hat.

She hit the button to send the window sliding down without unlocking the door, leaned across the seat, and smiled at him. "Hi. What's your name?"

He blinked at her and wiped his face with his sleeve. "Mason."

"Mason who?"

"Mason Yarrow," he gasped.

"Thanks, Mason," she said. "Hold it there for a moment." She activated the camera and took a photo, then went back to her conversation. "Did you get that? Mason Yarrow. I'm sending through a photo. I'll phone when I get to Lucky Luke's."

She terminated the call and punched the button to unlock the doors.

He opened the back door first and heaved his sack onto the seat. It sounded heavy. The back door slammed, and he finally clambered into the seat beside her, still breathing hard.

"Thank you." *Puff, puff.* "I thought I'd be still standing there come morning." His eyes went to her phone. "Sensible, taking a photo, telling someone what you were doing."

Georgie smiled at him, wondering if the next thing on the agenda would be to call the paramedics for a Santa Claus with a heart attack. "I'm only going as far as the next RV park, but if you can't get a ride, it's better than standing on the side of the road. That suit you?"

He nodded, still breathing hard.

"Would you like a drink of water?" She jerked a thumb over her shoulder to the back seat. "There's a six-pack back there."

"Don't mind if I do." Gratefully, he twisted his bulk around and stretched over with a grunt. Georgie eased the truck back onto the road and got rolling again, waiting until he had drunk his fill before she got to what she wanted to know.

"And the $64,000 question is... why is Santa Claus hitchhiking?" She grinned. "With your sack, no less. Someone steal your sleigh?"

He took his time answering, looking from her to

the road ahead, and finally shook his head. "Miss, I don't know where to start."

"How long have you been standing there with your thumb out?"

"Half an hour…maybe a bit more."

"Okay." Georgie waited, but he said nothing more. A glance to the side showed her that he was staring at the road ahead, his brow furrowed, while he played with the cap of the bottle of water.

"I'm on my way to join the family for Christmas," she said conversationally. "Over in Elkhart."

"Oh, yes?" His voice was polite but lacked genuine interest. "All staying in an RV park there, are you?"

She realized he thought she was part of a traveling gypsy family. "No. I'm staying at my father's house. I just live in this when I'm traveling."

"That's nice." He leaned back and closed his eyes, weariness in every bone.

Georgie's senses began to twitch. This happened sometimes, she noticed, since she had been doing readings with a crystal ball. It was as though her awareness had heightened generally—a kind of radar.

That radar was telling her that this was a man with more than an amusing story to tell about how Santa and his sack had ended up on the side of the road.

"I'm moving on to Omaha tomorrow, meeting my

partner there," she told him. "From there, it'll take a couple of days to get to Elkhart."

"Sounds good." His head lolled to the side, against the window, and he stared at the road unwinding ahead of them.

Georgie persisted. "Where are you headed?"

There was another pause before he sighed and said, "I was thinking Lincoln, to a friend of mine, but now… I'm not sure."

Taken aback, Georgie pondered where to go with this.

"Have you got a change of clothes in that sack?"

"No." A thread of humor entered his voice. "It really is full of Christmas presents. None of which are clothes, other than maybe Superhero outfits for kids, which wouldn't be much of an improvement."

"Mason…" Georgie was totally at a loss. She had a growing conviction that this was someone who needed help, but she didn't have a clue what kind of help and how to offer it.

Well, she wasn't a gypsy fortune teller for nothing. If anyone could find out what was going on here, surely she could.

Impulsively, she said, "Mason, if you're not in a hurry, would you like to join me for supper?"

That got his attention. His head rolled slowly back her way, and he studied her carefully. His pale blue eyes looked tired.

"I've got money for a meal," he said, "if that's what you're wondering."

"I wasn't sure," Georgie admitted, looking at the miles unrolling in front of her. The lights of a passing vehicle flashed by them. "But there's no store at the RV park. Look, you don't have to tell me what happened if you don't want to. But let me treat you to supper anyway. I've got a couple of steaks in the fridge, a bag of salad ready to toss. Nothing fancy."

She could sense his hesitation before he finally said, "Thank you. That's very nice of you. I accept." He mustered up a smile. "You should be safe, now that your friend has my photo ready to send out to police highway vehicles everywhere."

"I didn't have any doubt," she said.

She was positive that her hitchhiking Santa Claus didn't present any threat to her. He might, however, be yet another person who needed her specialized services. Even if he didn't know it yet.

Find it at your preferred bookstore or online: https://books2read.com/A-Rocking-Good-Christmas